MIGRANT!

The Story of Danny Broome

MARK GENGLER

Titles

by Mark Gengler

NOAH THORNE
A WISCONSIN FARM BOY IN THE 1920'S

THANKS A LOT GOD

WOLF CREEK CIDER
THE STORY OF AARON STROUD

MIGRANT!
THE STORY OF DANNY BROOME

*This novel is dedicated to my grand-parents,
my parents and all my Uncles and Aunts who lived through
and survived one of the worst periods of American history.*

*As a child, I remember them talking about a dollar a day
wages, pulling together to get by and praying things
would get better.*

*Their generation saw the banks close and neighbors
lose their farms. The Civilian Conservation Corps
helped my Father and Uncles to feed and cloth their families.*

*I thank each one of them for the values
they passed on to their children.*

MIGRANT!

The Story of Danny Broome

MARK GENGLER

CHRISTOPHER MATTHEWS PUBLISHING

MIGRANT! *The Story of Danny Broome*
by Mark Gengler

Published by

SOUL FIRE PRESS
PO Box 571
Gleneden Beach, OR 97388

The events, peoples and incidents in this story are the sole product of the author's imagination. The story is fictitious, and any resemblance to individuals, living or dead, is purely coincidental.

Interior layout, cover design by Suzanne Parrott
Cover art Shutterstock.com:
The old steam locomotive is driving. © Yarikart (ID 1282915756)

Genre: *Young Adult, stock market crash, depression Migrant workers, prohibition, bank robbery, farming, harvesting, southern United States, romance, friendship*

ISBN: 978-1-944072-53-7 (pb)

10 9 8 7 6 5 4 3 2 1

Printed in the
United States of America

ACKNOWLEDGMENTS

No author has ever written a novel alone. I owe many thank yous to many people. To Suzanne, my new publisher and editor who took the time to get to know me and give me much needed advice and help. My wife Mary the 'computer widow' when I really get into the meat of the story. To Kim, Maria, Jacob and Shelly who got me through some tough mornings with smiles and hot coffee. To my brother and sisters, nieces and nephews, cousins and their extended families who give me encouragement and ideas for the next novel. To my friends Reggie and Judy for just being there when I need a shoulder to lean on. All of you helped make this possible.

CHAPTER ONE

The bread and soup line seems to get longer every morning. More jobs gone, more men out of work, and more families going hungry. Last year, 1929, the stock market crashed, and the whole country went belly up. My name is Danny Broome, and I worked for the Compton Coal Company delivering fifty-pound bags of coal to homes in the Bronx, New York. I stand almost six feet tall and can carry a bag of coal on each shoulder. My dark hair and dark hazel eyes let you know I am an Irishman.

It's mid-April 1930 with no two days alike. Yesterday was sunshine and sixty degrees; today, it's drizzling rain and about forty degrees. I pull my thin jacket tighter. Standing behind me, my friend Paulie pokes my ribs and then points at a guy walking down the line, passing out handbills.

"I wonder what he's selling?" Paulie asked.

I grabbed one of the bills and read it. "Some people in Plum, Pennsylvania needs help planting potatoes and carrots."

"I can't go. I got a wife and kid to look after."

I was single, my folks died during the flu epidemic, and my one older sister, Amy, was married to a cop in Queens. "I'll check it out," I told Paulie. "I got nothing keeping me here."

I was living out of the Mission House on Decatur Street. I gave them money when I got work, which was becoming a daily challenge. Getting out of the city might just be a good move.

The handbill said a bus was leaving Union Station on Tuesday morning at eight o'clock for Plum. By Monday afternoon, I had decided to go. Everything I owned fit in an old canvas satchel with room to spare. A second pair of pants, a change of underwear, and a flannel shirt was the total wealth of this twenty-two-year-old. I shook hands with the older man who ran the Mission and informed him about the job.

"Take this with you," he said as he handed me a pocket-sized Bible. "Just something to read on your journey." Raised a Catholic, I had not set foot in a church since Dad's funeral—that was ten years ago. I thanked him, putting the Bible in the satchel, and left.

Twenty people were waiting for the bus. Most were guys like me, some younger, some older. A couple, in their mid-sixties, were turned away. She had a rasping cough, and he could barely walk with a cane. A cop scanned the worn and desperate faces, possibly looking for a robbery suspect.

Eighteen people boarded the old bus, and I settled in for a long ride, sitting next to a guy named John. He smelled like cheap gin, but his eyes were clear.

"Hell of a way to live," he offered, then pulled his hat down over his eyes. I took the Bible out of my satchel and opened it to Psalms. After about an hour, I nodded off.

The driver pulled off the road about noon, passed back a paper sack three-quarters full of cheese sandwiches, then drove on. I watched the countryside roll by as I ate. It was different seeing fields and trees instead of tall buildings. A few farmers were out working the fields, probably planting. By late afternoon the bus arrived at a large farm. A big two-story house sat in the middle of a collection of smaller buildings. We all climbed down from the bus and waited in the gravel drive. A tall man with a beard stepped out of the house and walked down to us.

"My name is Emmett Castle. I farm five-hundred acres of produce here, mostly potatoes, carrots and cabbage. Your wages are a dollar a day. We start planting tomorrow." Another man walked up and nodded his head. "This is my foreman, Hal Decker," Mr. Castle said. "He will get you settled in the bunkhouse and take you to the cook shack. Fill your bellies and get a good night's sleep."

We awoke at 6 a.m., and after a breakfast of oatmeal and coffee, Decker organized us into groups. I was assigned to planting potatoes. It was mindless work: dig a small hole, drop in a potato eye, cover the hole. We stopped at noon for sandwiches and coffee bought out by truck, then continued planting until sundown.

Supper consisted of beef stew, cornbread, and more coffee. We took turns using the shower, and I hand-washed my socks and underwear. At the rate we were going, I calculated the crops should all be planted in about three weeks, working six days a week. That would glean me $18 in wages. Then, an older guy named Arnie told us, "I heard some of these farmers deduct money from your wages for food and board. I don't know if this guy does, but be warned."

As we came in from the fields on the third Saturday, Mr. Castle was there to meet us. "I need a dozen workers to work Sunday to get the carrots in. I'll pay two dollars per man. The rest of you come up to the house and draw your pay." Ten of us stepped forward; the rest headed for the house.

By Sunday afternoon, the carrots were all planted. Good to his word, Mr. Castle handed us each two dollars.

"Hal will take you into Plum tomorrow morning to catch the bus," he said, "and if you are around about mid-September, stop by. I'll need good help for the harvest."

At the station, many of the workers went looking for a speakeasy. Since prohibition, I had lost my taste for booze. Instead, I asked the guy in the ticket office if there a second-hand clothing store close by.

Pointing to his left, he replied, "Head down two blocks to St. Peters church. They got a basement full of stuff."

An elderly gentleman led me to the church basement. I rummaged through the trove of clothing, finding a fine pair of work boots to replace my old wore out shoes, a pair of good jeans, a cotton shirt, and some socks.

The man scrutinized the bundle. "It all comes to two dollars."

"Is there a clean rooming house around?" I asked, handing him the bills.

Looking me over carefully, he said, "I have a room I can rent to you. How long will you be staying?"

"Just till I find work." He wrote down the address and handed it to me.

"The house is a block from here on Waters Avenue. I'm William Finch and I'll be home around four o'clock."

I shook his hand. "I'm Danny Broome and I will see you at four."

William was a widower and a fine cook: meatloaf, mashed potatoes and gravy, and coffee.

"My wife Grace died from cancer three years ago," he said, "and our son is married and lives in Scranton. He works for Standard Oil Company. I only see him and his wife Alice at Christmas."

I told him about life in the Bronx and working at the potato farm. "I'll be out all day tomorrow looking for more work." I said, running my hand through my hair. "Is there a barbershop around here?" He told me where and I said good night.

Outside a union hall on 29th Street, I noticed a man with a clipboard talking to people. H looked at me as I approached.

"I'm looking for some men to do shovel work on a road crew. You interested?"

"What's the pay?" I asked.

"Dollar-fifty a day. Job should last a week." He handed me a yellow card. "A bus will pick you up at the station tomorrow at 7 a.m. Show this card."

There were eight of us there the following morning. The bus ride took about half an hour. I had shoveled coal, so this wasn't much different. After five days, the job was done.

After drawing my pay, I thanked William for the room and handed him three dollars. We shook hands, and I headed toward the bus station, unsure what I would do next. I decided to ponder my decision with a coffee at the food stand. That's when I met Wiley Bishop.

CHAPTER TWO

As I paid for the coffee, a voice behind me asked, "Could you possibly buy this poor broke Irishman a coffee?"

I turned and handed him my cup and then smiled. "From one Irishman to another."

Except for the dark red hair, we could have been brothers—close to six-foot, broad-chested with hazel eyes. We walked outside and sat on the bench and exchanged life stories.

Wiley was from Trenton, New Jersey. He had two sisters; one was married. His mother had died five years ago from diabetes, his father was in prison for assaulting a judge. I inquired as to why anyone would beat up a judge. With a wink and a smile, he replied, "Because the bastard deserved it."

He asked what I was doing in Plum, so I told him about the potato farm. "How would you like to head down to Georgia and pick some cucumbers?" he asked.

"Some warmer weather would suit me fine," I said, "but how do you know there is really work?"

"Another guy put me onto it last year Now I follow the migrant harvesters around the country. It's not a bad living if you're single."

"How do we get there?" I asked.

"The bus ticket costs $2.50. Can you get two? I'll pay you back later," Wiley said.

The bus left at two that afternoon for Shelbyville, Georgia. Wiley was a talker with some great stories. One involved a man named Boolie, who had a goat for sale. The goat would run away from the new owner back to Boolie, who would sell it again. Once, after a week, the goat had not returned to Boolie, so he went to the new owner to find out why.

"We ate it," the man told him. "Had a family cookout." Boolie spent a week in jail for attacking the man with a club.

At a regular stop in North Carolina, we had an hour while the bus gassed up and took on a few passengers. We got sandwiches and coffee from a vendor then got aboard. I slept off and on as the miles rolled by in the night. I woke when Wiley poked me in the ribs. The sun was just coming up as we pulled into the station. "All out for Shelbyville," the driver hollered.

We got a ride in the back of an old pick-up truck with a guy and his wife who were there to pick up another guy.

"We're going to the James' brothers farm," Wiley told me. "They got a couple hundred acres of cucumbers to pick. If they got enough pickers, it'll take about a week."

"What's the pay?" I asked.

"The usual, a dollar a day, but the food is good."

At the farm, we bunked in a small cabin with an older guy named Frank from Ohio. That's how he introduced himself. "Hi fellas, I'm Frank from Ohio." We introduced ourselves and asked how long he had been on the road.

"I guess I been doing this for three years. I try to stay in the south—me and cold weather don't get along to well. This is my third year at this place. They treat you pretty good."

"Some of the wives work in the cook shack," Wiley said, referring to the migrant families, "while most of the kids work in the field. You would be surprised how fast those little hands can pick cucumbers."

Three stake-bed trucks drove in, one loaded with baskets. People began climbing in the trucks, so Wiley and I hopped aboard. A man with a clipboard came around, taking down our names. He waved at the driver and yelled, "Take them out!"

It was the first week of May, and the Georgia sun was hard at work. The baskets filled quickly and were hauled to the end of the rows where trucks picked them up. Sandwiches and cold water for lunch, then we picked till sundown. I learned that bending over to pick killed your back. You had to squat and shuffle your feet as you went. By the time we quit for the day, I was hungry and exhausted.

The food was good, just as Frank had said. I ate till I couldn't hold any more, washing it down with iced tea. Afterward, a few of the younger women smiled and winked at me, but I just smiled back and kept walking toward the cabin. I didn't need some angry father or brother chasing me with a knife.

Wiley and Frank were talking about the next stop. "There's a big cabbage farm just outside of Winnsboro, Louisiana," Frank told us. "It's run by a family named Saltere. They got clean cabins and about 300 acres of cabbages to pick."

We talked it over, then Frank said, "Pete Jenks and his family will give us a ride in the back of their truck. They go there every year."

By the end of the week, the cukes were all picked, and my blisters were becoming calluses. Saturday afternoon, after we got paid, we looked up Pete Jenks.

"The family and I will spend the night here, then go to Church in Shelbyville in the morning," he told us. "I'll pick you boys up at the bus station about noon." Wiley and I got a ride into town to do some shopping and find a room for the night.

CHAPTER THREE

We found a second-hand store and stocked up on clothes. I just threw away some of my old clothes. Wiley saw some pocket knives in a glass case, and we each bought a Case knife. A Fedora hat in almost new condition fit me perfectly.

Walking down Butler Avenue, we saw a sign: ROOMS FOR RENT. The older lady behind the desk let us have a room with two beds and a bathroom with a shower at the end of the hall. I hadn't shaved in a week, and it felt great to get all cleaned up.

Dressed in our *new* used clothes, we got a fifty-cent meal at a diner and then went to a movie. Jimmy Cagney was on the run and shooting it out with dozens of cops.

Back at the rooming house, I told Wiley, "After the cabbages, I am pretty sure I'm done with vegetables for a while."

"I know what you mean," he said. "I've been seeing cucumbers in my sleep."

We met Pete, his wife Dolores, their two boys, and Frank at noon. Dolores noticed our different clothes and asked, "Where is that store?" We took them there and waited while she and the boys did some shopping. There was a big smile on her face when she came out. Frank even bought a new hat. Then we loaded up and headed for Louisiana.

The younger boy, Sam, was seven years old and sat in the cab with his folks. The older boy, Delbert, was ten years old and rode in the back with us. We were sitting on a mattress covered with a blanket when the boy opened a wooden box and took out a sack of salted peanuts. Spreading out a big blue handkerchief, he warned, "Don't get no shells on the mattress. Pa gets real mad about that."

We had to drive across Alabama and Mississippi to get to Louisiana. "Pa tried sharecropping in Mississippi," Delbert said, "but we darn near starved to death. We picked cotton until our fingers was bleeding, then the owner told Pa he couldn't pay cause he was broke. That's when we went on the road."

Wiley and I paid for gas in Mississippi. It might have been cheaper going by bus, but as long as the salted peanuts held out, I was happy. Wednesday afternoon, we crossed the Louisiana border, and by evening we arrived at the Saltere farm. Pete and Dolores had been here before and parked in front of a small house. "This is where we stay," Pete said. "You folks can stay in the bunkhouse. Frank knows the way."

After breakfast, Emery Saltere came around to sign us up. "My son Calvin is the foreman, he will take you out to the field and get you started." I learned real quick that cabbages are heavy. A worker came by, dropping off boxes to be filled. Then another crew came behind, loading the filled boxes into trucks. A short lunch break, then more cabbages until sundown.

Frank was right again; the food was excellent. A big pan of pulled pork, homemade bread, and baked potatoes. The iced tea was so sweet it hurt my teeth, but I drank all I could hold. Wiley bummed a cigarette off of someone and lit up. I had never gotten into the smoking habit because of the cost. "I smoke once in a while," Wiley said, "but not often enough to buy a pack."

It took us ten days to clear the field. By Saturday afternoon, the last truck hauled away the last cabbages. As we came in from the field, there was a table set up in the yard. Emery's wife, Lucerne, sat there with a cash box and clipboard in front of her. Calvin stood behind her with a big pistol stuck in his belt. Lucerne asked for our name, checked it off, and handed out two five-dollar bills to each worker. Wiley and I said goodbye to Pete, Dolores and Frank and got on the truck going into Winnsboro.

CHAPTER FOUR

Wiley and I found a run-down hotel in town that charged fifty cents a night for a bed. "There's a diner down the block, let's get a coffee," I said.

As we walked down the sidewalk, Wiley asked, "So, got an idea where do we go from here?"

"If we don't think about it too hard, something will turn up," I said with little hope.

"Just so it don't involve cabbages," Wiley said with a sigh.

We sat at the counter sipping hot, bitter coffee and chatting with the waitress. Her name was Janet. She was about thirty-five years old, brown hair, brown eyes, divorced, and her feet hurt. We learned all this because Janet was starved for conversation.

"You boys must be passing through. I know most of the regulars. What brings you here?"

"We just finished harvesting cabbages at the Saltere farm," I told her. "Now we need to find more work."

Scratching behind her ear with a pencil, she said, "I saw in yesterday's newspaper that farmers in Claremore, Oklahoma need help putting up their first crop hay. The migrants are busy picking vegetables; they don't much care for cutting hay." We left her a dollar tip and walked to the bus station.

A bus-route map took up half of one wall. The highway went up into Arkansas, cut across the state's southwest corner, and into Oklahoma.

"How much to Claremore, Oklahoma?" Wiley asked the ticket clerk.

Flipping open his book, the clerk ran his finger down the list. "One way to Claremore is 75 cents. Bus leaves at 6 a.m."

The bus rolled in, pulling to a stop at the station platform at 5:45 the next morning. The door jerked open, and the driver stood, stepped back one row of seats, and hauled a man out by his collar.

The ticket clerk came rushing out of his office. "What's going on?"

"This damn drunk threw up in the aisle," said the driver as he threw the drunk onto the ground. "I have to clean it up before anyone gets on or off." The drunk started to crawl away down the platform.

"I'll get a bucket and some rags," sighed the clerk.

Shaking his head, the driver reached inside and tossed out an old canvas-covered canteen. Wiley picked it up, pulled the cork, and sniffed. He looked at me with a smirk saying, "I know moonshine when I smell it."

I smiled as the bus motored through Arkansas. Growing up in the Bronx had not prepared me for all this open country. We stopped twice to pick up passengers. A woman with a young girl got on and took the seats across the aisle.

Looking over at us, the woman said, "If you boys are hungry, I've got some sandwiches." She passed over two bologna and cheese sandwiches.

"Thank you kindly ma'am, we didn't expect to eat until we got to Oklahoma."

"Are you looking for work?" she asked.

"We heard they need help with the first-crop hay," Wiley said, "so we are going to Claremore."

The lady started laughing and clapped her hands together. "Trust in the Lord, and He shall provide," she said happily. "I'm Millie Bouchard, this is my daughter Angie. My husband Eldon and I own the Circle D Ranch five miles outside of Claremore."

"My name is Wiley Bishop and my friend here is Danny Broome," he told her. "We sure could use the work."

"Angie and I are coming back from visiting my sister's in Arkansas," Millie said, "hoping her two sons could help with the hay, but both of them got picked up for running moonshine. If you boys want work, we sure got it!"

Eldon Bouchard was waiting at the bus station. Millie was laughing as she told him the story about her nephews and meeting us.

"Get in the car and let's go home," said Eldon. "I've got a month's work for both of you. Just to let you know, Millie is the best cook in the county. You'll sleep in the bunkhouse, but you eat with us."

We told Eldon we had never done this kind of work. With a big grin, he said, "If you can handle a pitchfork without stabbing each other, you'll catch on the first day. What kind of work have you been doing?"

"Harvesting cucumbers and cabbages," I told him.

"This work you can do standing up," Eldon said. "Just stacking hay on the wagon."

It was late afternoon when we got to the ranch. Three men were washing up at the pump in the yard.

"Come on over, and I'll introduce you to my crew," Eldon said. The older of the three was Charley, then Fred, maybe in his mid-thirties, and finally Joe, a Native American about our age. "Fellas, these boys will be helping us. Take them to the bunkhouse and get them settled, then time for supper."

Wiley and I introduced ourselves as we all walked to the bunkhouse. Charley was the talker, telling us, "Eldon does the cutting with a mowing machine and also does the windrows. I drive the tractor with the hay-loader, young Joe there has been piling it on the wagon and Fred puts it in the haymow."

"I noticed two other wagons in the yard," I said. "Do we use those too?"

Fred chimed in. "When the wagon is full, you unhook the loader, Charley drives it to the barn. There you unhook the full wagon and you hook on an empty wagon, then back to the field. You'll catch on quick."

Looking around, I asked Charley, "Where are the horses?"

"They're all out to pasture now," he said. "Otherwise they would be in the way."

We rose early the following day. After a breakfast of hot cinnamon rolls and coffee, Wiley and I hooked up an empty wagon to the Case tractor and climbed on. Eldon was already windrowing. It had been a warm breezy night, and the hay was dry. Charley backed the wagon up to the hay-loader and showed us how to hook it up. As he drove, the hay came up over the top of the loader and down into the wagon.

As the wagon filled, Charley was yelling, "Stomp it down, Stomp it down!" When we thought the wagon was full, Charley knew better. "Stomp it down," he yelled over the noise of the tractor. When Charley finally stopped, the load of hay was a little higher than the loader. Charley unhooked the loader and headed back to the barn.

Charley stopped the wagon under a thick overhead beam with a big four-pronged rig on a pulley. Fred told us how to open the rig and stomp the prongs into the hay inside the mow. Then we stood back as a load of hay went up and into the mow, where Joe spread it around and then stomped it down.

Angie walked over from the house carrying a jug of water and a straw hat. She handed Charley the water and Wiley the hat. "You gotta wear this or the sun will cook your head."

Wiley took the hat with a smile and said, "Thank you, I will wear it every day from now on."

Now that our training was over, Charley split us up. I worked in the field with Charley, and Wiley helped Joe in the mow. Then we would switch.

"It gets awful hot in that mow," Charley said. "This way all three of you get a breather." We still would be stomping but in different places.

By sundown, the mow was full. Not another forkful of hay would fit inside. As if he knew what I was going to ask, Charley spoke up. "Good work boys. Tomorrow we start stacking hay in the field for the winter."

We washed up at the pump and went to supper. In the summer, the Bouchard's and all the workers ate at a big picnic table in the backyard. Millie had a big pot of chicken and dumplings, dishes of green beans and potatoes, bread, and iced tea. Later, I borrowed a pencil and paper and wrote to my sister, Amy, telling her what I had been doing and where I was. I tucked a five-dollar bill in, knowing they could use it. Angie offered to mail it for me.

CHAPTER FIVE

By the third week, I finally saw the horses. We were loading hay on the last field when Charley stopped the tractor and pointed to his left. There must have been over a dozen, ranging in color from light tan to dark brown and a few pintos. I climbed down from the wagon then Charley and I headed over to the fence. One of the horses nickered and walked up to Charley. He reached out scratched her head.

"This is Belle," said Charley. "She is one of the brood mares and Angie's favorite." I reached out and petted her neck. Pointing at her large belly, Charley smiled. "She's in foal, that means she will be giving us another one, probably this fall."

The first of June fell on a Friday, not a cloud in the sky, and the sun was beating down as we made the last stack. We climbed onto the wagon, and Charley drove us back to the barn. Wiley and I had become friends with Charley, Fred, and Joe. We learned that Joe was an orphan who had wandered in two years ago looking for work. At first, Eldon thought Joe was too young and skinny to be much help, but Angie said, "He just needs a family," so he got hired. "I will work here as long as they will have me," he told us.

Friday was payday, and after supper, Eldon handed Wiley and me each an envelope. Inside we each found a ten and two fives. As we shook Eldon's hand, Millie came out of the house and said

"I got a letter Tuesday from my brother Jason Bender in Hazelton, Kansas." She took the letter from her apron, opened it, and read, "We are just starting our wheat harvest and good help is scarce this year." She folded the letter putting it back in her apron pocket. "I wrote back to Jason letting him know that we had two strong boys who might be heading his way. Are you interested?"

Grinning broadly, Wiley asked, "Can I take my straw hat with me?"

Nodding her blonde head, she smiled. "Only if you wear it every day."

Millie drove us to town Saturday morning, dropping us off at the train station. "The train will take you right into Hazelton and it's an hour faster than the bus," she said. We thanked her, and she waved as she drove off.

We each had a dollar in our pocket, heeding old Charley's advice. "If you're traveling by bus or train these days," he said, wagging a finger, "keep your money in your boot. Times is tough, and there's people out there that ain't as honest as you." The ticket was a dollar, and the clerk told us it was about a four-hour ride.

The passenger car was half full when we got on board. A middle-aged man with a scraggly beard smelling of booze took up the first two seats. The remainder of the car, filling from back to front, included four nuns traveling together, several families with school-age children, and a farmer and his son. Wiley and I took seats about five rows from the front. A well-dressed man in a suit and bowler hat sat in front and across the aisle from us. Then, the conductor walked down the aisle punching tickets, and the train jerked to a start.

The first hour, we watched as the flat fields rolled by. Wiley sat by the window and soon nodded off to sleep. I took out the pocket Bible and started reading Proverbs.

"Everybody! I want to see those hands in the air!" I jerked back to see the man with the scraggly beard holding a revolver in his right hand and a cloth bag in his left. "Turn out your pockets and put the money in the bag," he ordered. "I want watches too, but no damn rings!" He jabbed the farmer in the back with the gun. "I know you got a watch, put it in the bag!" People didn't have much, but it was all taken.

By the time he got to me, Wiley was wide awake. We had pulled out our pants pockets which were empty.

"Stand up boys," he snarled, checking our hip pockets and then taking off our hats looking inside. "Deadbeats," he mumbled, tossing our hats to the ground. When he reached the man in the bowler hat, he poked the gentleman with the revolver then pointed it back in the air. I was angry at this bandit, and without thinking, I slipped into the aisle, took a step, and tackled him! He gave a half scream, half holler as he went down with my full weight on his back.

The hand hit the floor, and the gun went skittering down the aisle. Wiley jumped over both of us and grabbed it. When the robber looked up, Wiley was sitting on the floor, pointing the gun in his face! The bowler hat guy removed his necktie, which we used to tie the thief's hands while the farmer's son went to find the conductor.

Everybody wanted their stuff back, so I said, "Let the conductor see all this first so Jesse James here can't lie his way out of it." Agreeing with that idea, they settled down, grumbling about the robber.

The conductor located an off-duty policeman from Hazelton in the next car. He came back and took the guy and the gun. "You folks can all have your belongings back, just write down what he stole and sign it," he said. He also took a statement from Wiley and me, laughing and shaking his head as he wrote.

"I got a friend works for the Hazelton newspaper," he said, "If you guys don't mind, I'm gonna give him this story. Folks like it when good guys take down the bad guys."

Franklin P. Dowd was the man in the bowler hat. He was a bank examiner on his way to Lincoln, Nebraska.

"Losing a hundred dollars would have been bad," he said, thanking us. "But losing the watch that once belonged to my grandfather would have been devastating. How can I thank you?" He offered us a reward, but we turned him down.

Always thinking, Wiley offered, "We haven't eaten all day. Maybe a good meal in Hazelton would be in order."

"I will gladly buy you both the best steak in town," said Franklin with a big smile. The rest of the passengers shook our hands and slapped our backs. The nuns blessed us several times, and the conductor wrote down our names, asking where we could be reached. We gave him the address of Jason Bender. By the time the excitement died down, the train had pulled into the Hazelton station.

CHAPTER SIX

At one o'clock that afternoon, Franklin P. Dowd ushered us into the dining room at the Hazelton Hotel. Emily, the waitress, took our order, and then Franklin asked her the cost.

"Two steaks, baked potatoes, bread and coffee with dessert comes to five dollars." Opening his wallet, Franklin handed her seven dollars. Her eyes opened as wide as her mouth. "I never got a two dollar tip before," she gasped.

Laughing and smiling, Franklin said, "It's a very special day." He then shook our hands and left to catch the train to Lincoln.

The dessert was apple pie, which was pretty good. As we finished our coffee, we asked Emily for directions to the Bender farm. We stood to leave when an older man walked in.

Pointing at us, he said, "You guys caught the robber on the train, right?"

"Yes sir, we did," I answered.

With a big smile, he held out his hand. "I'm George Newcomb. I own the town newspaper. It comes out every week on Wednesday. I sure would like to take your picture and print your story, if you can spare some time."

Sensing an opportunity, Wiley said, "We're on our way to the Bender farm to find work."

"If you give me the scoop on the robbery, I'll have someone drive you out to the farm," said George. Rubbing my chin and thinking for a minute, I agreed.

After the interview, an older woman from the office drove us out to the farm. We had to tell her the story in more detail on the way out. She giggled and gasped and said "oh my Lord" several times as Wiley embellished the tale. Dropping us in the driveway, she promised to have a paper delivered on Wednesday.

Jason Bender was a tall, barrel-chested man who crushed your hand when he shook it. "Millie wrote that you boys might be headed this way. Well, I've got work for you." He pointed out to a field where a huge metal machine on wheels was sitting. "The threshing machine arrived this morning. It will take all afternoon to get everything set up, then Monday morning we start work."

He walked us over to the bunkhouse. "Pick out a bunk and get settled. Pay is a dollar a day. My foreman, Louie Soames, will be by to sign you in." Taking some empty bunks in the back, we agreed not to tell anyone about the train robbery. They would find out soon enough.

Sunday, we relaxed and met the other workers. Most were in their thirties and forties and had done farming their whole life. Now they followed the thresher just to stay alive. They told us how it was done and what to expect.

One of the guys, Orin, noticed Wiley's long hair and offered to cut it for fifty cents. "You can pay me later," he offered, so Wiley sat on a chair outside while Orin worked away with a comb and scissors.

When he felt the job was done, he handed Wiley a mirror. "Thanks," Wiley said. "It looks a lot better." I had to agree. Orin had done a good job.

Sunday evening, we all ate at some plank tables with benches under the trees: homemade biscuits, bowls of chicken casserole, peas, carrots, and macaroni, washed down with iced tea. The men talked about past harvests and the lack of rain.

"We are in a drought year," Jason said. "With no rain forecast at all, this could be our only harvest this year."

Foreman Louie Soames spoke up. "What scares me is those dust storms west of us." All nodded their heads, murmuring in agreement.

"What dust storms?" Wiley asked. Louie then told us about the scourge of the plains.

"Around 1900, a lot of farmers from the east were running out of land to plant. They heard about the homesteads being given away out west." I moved a bit closer so I wouldn't miss anything. "The great prairie stretches from the Mississippi river to the Rocky Mountains," said Louie waving his arm. "Farmers came with plows and turned the prairie into farmland."

"It sure helped out those soldiers over in Europe during the Great War," said Jason.

"Yes it did," Louie said. "Tons of wheat, corn and oats were harvested. But with each crop the plows loosened the topsoil. The rains came every year and we continued plowing and planting."

Another man spoke up. "We haven't had a good rain in over two years."

"Now, the north Canadian wind picks up the loose dusty topsoil and forms massive dust storms," Louie said, "and those storms are getting closer to us all the time."

A silent nodding of heads let me know this was a very serious threat to their lively-hood. Soon after, it was time to get some rest for the big day tomorrow. Before we crawled into our bunks, one of the old-timers said, "Best to shake out your blankets before you lay down. Lots of field mice around." Everybody shook their blankets, but no mice.

I was asleep as soon as my head hit the pillow.

CHAPTER SEVEN

The grain-binder was a strange-looking machine. A big paddle wheel sat on top of a wood and metal frame holding a canvas apron. As the binder cut the stalks of wheat, they fell onto the apron and then fed into a covered box-like structure that rolled the wheat into a bundle and dropped it on the ground. A team of horses pulling a wagon followed. Our job was to fork the bundles onto the wagon. When the wagon was full, it went to the threshing machine, where two more men forked the piles into the maw of the noisy belt-driven machine.

The thresher was steam-driven, and when the water level got low, a whistle sounded. Another team of horses hauled milk cans full of water to be poured into the tank on the side of the thresher. Now came the process of separating the wheat from the chaff. Grain blew into a waiting truck while dumping the chaff on the ground by the thresher. The truck hauled the wheat to Hazelton's Grain Plant & Silo to be bagged and tagged for Bender Farms.

The thresher's whistle sounded, and everything shut down for the noon meal. The horses were unharnessed and watered, and the men stood around the pump washing off the chaff that covered everyone. The plank tables were laden with platters of chicken, bowls of mashed potatoes, gravy, green beans, and sliced bread. Pitchers of water, milk, tea, and a big pot of coffee sat among the feast. Jason's wife, Ingrid, and teen-aged daughter, Nancy, kept the tables supplied, and when I thought we were done, slices of apple pie appeared. Wiley got two pieces of pie and a broad wink from Nancy.

"It must be the haircut she likes," Wiley said with a smile.

When things are going along smoothly, something is bound to happen. About two o'clock, the big long belt driving the thresher slid off of the pulley, flew backward, and slapped the nose of one of the horses pulling the water wagon. The team bolted. Cans of water went flying everywhere. One of the men got in front of the team and managed to grab their bridles, dragging him ten feet before he managed to pull their heads down and stop them. No one had been injured, but the thresher had to be shut down while the belt was replaced. In an hour, we were back up and running. Pick up the bundle, toss it in the wagon. Pick up the bundle, toss it in the wagon. It was mindless work, but it was also important because it would feed families for months to come.

Wednesday, the noon whistle blew, and we all gathered around the pump in the yard washing up. Young Nancy came running out of the house yelling and waving the newspaper.

"They're heroes, they really are heroes! They stopped the train robbery!"

Jason bender took the paper from his daughter and saw our picture taking up half the front page. "Well, I'll be damned! You boys really are heroes!" He passed the paper around as we walked to the plank tables. A lot more handshaking and backslapping took place as we sat down to eat.

Ingrid came from the house with tears in her eyes. "Those nuns were from our church," she sniffled and gave us both a hug. Wiley told the story again with a few more embellishments, and I actually heard my name mentioned twice.

That afternoon, we finished field number one, and the thresher moved to field number two. By noon Saturday, Jason Bender's winter wheat crop was harvested. Louie Sames came around later with a cashbox and paid the men six dollars each.

"This came in the mail for you," he said, handing me a letter. It was from the President of the Atchison, Topeka & Santa Fe Railroad Company. I opened it, and Wiley and I read it together. He thanked us at length for putting our lives at risk to protect the safety of the passengers on the train.

"To show our gratitude," he wrote, "you will find enclosed two Gold rail passes good for three months anywhere in the United States to be used and reused at your convenience." We just stood there staring at each other, then started laughing. It was crazy! This was happening to us, two migrant Irishmen able to travel anywhere we wished for three months!

When the excitement wore off, we sat down on a bunk and seemed to arrive at the same point.

"I want to go back to New York and see my sister," I told Wiley.

"Both of my sisters live in Trenton," he said. "Mattie, the oldest, has two boys who would like to see their favorite uncle." We shook on it and gathered up our things to catch a ride into town.

Wiley handed Orin a dollar for the haircut on the way out, and with a wink, he said, "Keep the change."

"The next one is free," Orin replied with a grin.

CHAPTER EIGHT

Earl, the ticket clerk in Hazelton, was thrilled to see us. He held up copies of newspapers from New York, Boston, Chicago, and Pittsburgh.

"Your story went nationwide," he said. "George Newcomb sent it to a friend in Chicago, and after all the bad news stories, this good news just caught on."

We showed him our gold tickets. "Are these really good for any rail line, like Burlington Northern or Milwaukee Road?"

Earl explained. "All the Railroad executives use them. Keep that letter you got handy, so the conductor knows you didn't steal them." On the station map, Earl outlined our travel to Trenton and on to New York. "The conductor will let you know when to switch trains and where."

The journey to New York was something seldom experienced by two young Irishmen. All the conductors but one knew who we were. They wanted their picture taken with us, and the sandwiches and coffee never ran out. When we switched trains in Chicago, a newspaper reporter was there. He rode with us to Indiana, furiously taking notes as we told him how we came to be in Kansas. He kept saying, "This is great, this is just great!"

We tried to impress on him the life of migrant workers. "I'm going to write a separate piece about them," he said, "because the nation needs to know."

In Pittsburgh, we switched trains again on the way to Trenton, New Jersey. Scenes of trees and fields changed to factories and smokestacks. After the open plains, it seemed like entering a foreign country. Wiley and I agreed to meet at the Trenton train station in one week at noon. We both knew we liked the traveling life, the new places, and the people.

From New York's busy train station, I took a bus to Queens that dropped me off a block from my sister's house. Amy had been blessed with red hair, green eyes, and a slender figure. She had taken care of me after mom died, raising me like a son. She had married Irish, a rookie cop named Thomas O'Riley, who adored her. I knocked on the door to the small one-story house. Amy opened the door, stared at me for a minute, then her hands flew to her face as her eyes opened wide.

"Oh my God, Danny!" she screamed and threw her arms around me. We were laughing and crying as we hugged each other. This was my family, and it was good to be home.

"You look so different," she kept saying. "You're all muscles and tan as an old leather belt!"

"Working in the sun will do that," I told her. She ran to the kitchen and got the newspaper she had been reading. On the front page was the picture of Wiley and me. "Thomas is so proud of you," she said. "He tells everyone he knows 'that's my brother-in-law!' He'll be home this evening and will be so glad to see you."

I told her about Wiley and all the places we'd been. She

thanked me for the letter and the money. "I must make something special for supper. Is spaghetti and meatballs still your favorite?"

My mouth watered. "I haven't had that since I left New York. Maybe some garlic bread too?"

Thomas O'Riley was born to be a policeman. His grandfather, father, and two uncles were all cops. Six feet tall, dark hair, blue eyes, and as quick with a smile as he was with his fists. He did not drink, smoke or gamble. Amy knew how to pick a husband. A big hug and broad smile were my greetings.

"Danny Broome, the hero of Hazelton!" he shouted so all the neighbors would hear. "Traveling suits you, you look fit and more."

Amy was an excellent cook, and I ate like a starving dog. We talked about the depression and what it had done to the city. Crime was on the rise—desperate men doing desperate things, like robbery and burglary.

"The speakeasies are full every night with hoodlums and whores for customers," Thomas told us. "I don't know where all the illegal whiskey is coming from, but there is no shortage of the vile stuff."

Thomas and Amy were members of Saint Andrews Catholic two blocks away. "Once a week, usually Saturday, we have a soup kitchen open at the church." Amy said, "It makes certain the children are being fed."

They told me that jobs were scarce. "You were wise to leave to find work, even though I worry about you." Amy said softly. "I'm glad you have a friend to travel with."

I told them about Wiley Bishop. "You never have to worry as long as we stay together."

After supper, I took a bath as Amy gathered up all my clothes. "You can wear some of Thomas's clothes while I wash and mend yours," she said. I slept on the sofa and woke the next morning to the smell of brewing coffee.

The washing machine in the kitchen was churning away as Amy kissed Thomas goodbye as he left to catch the bus to work. I hung the clothes out to dry on the line in the small backyard as Amy sat at the kitchen table writing a grocery list. "You can walk me to the market and help carry home the food," she said.

The market sat directly across the street from the church. Several of Amy's friends were there, and she introduced me as 'my brother who stopped the train robbery.' It was a point of pride for her that the Broome family name be upheld. I just said hello, smiled, and tipped my hat.

A separate bag was filled with vegetables and dropped off at the church, where I met Father Walters, the pastor, a middle-aged man with sad eyes and already gray hair. The basement kitchen was busy with ladies chopping vegetables, baking bread, and talking about their families. *This is what I miss being on the road,* I thought—*the sense of belonging, the security of a home, and the bonds of close friends.*

That evening I told Thomas and Amy of meeting Wiley in Trenton on Sunday at noon. Amy was sad I would miss church service. I showed her my pocket Bible.

"I read from it whenever I can," I said. "It's not church, but it eases my mind."

"Is Wiley Catholic?" Amy asked.

"I've never asked. But I think he might be. Perhaps someday I will ask him."

CHAPTER NINE

I was waiting on the platform when Wiley arrived. He stepped down from the passenger car, turned, and helped a young lady step down. He looked around, waved when he saw me ,and walked over with the young lady.

"Remember when I told you I had two sisters," he asked. "Mattie, is home with my nephews. This is my younger sister Kate, who insisted on meeting you."

Kate took my breath away: five foot eight inches tall, wavy black hair, emerald green eyes, slender but a filled-out figure, the pale Irish complexion, and a lovely smile. Without waiting for a handshake, she hugged me.

"I am so glad Wiley has you to travel with. I no longer worry about him constantly, just occasionally." Holding me at arms-length, she remarked, "You are as handsome as Wiley said you were."

Wiley was quietly laughing. "I must warn you, Kate is not shy. Also, I promised to buy her a root beer. Let's find a café."

I hadn't said a word. So awestruck, I wasn't sure I could speak without mumbling.

"Where are you two going this time," Kate asked, sipping her cold root beer.

"I'm thinking about Indiana," I said, finally finding my voice. "We saw a lot of hay-fields ready for harvest there."

"As long as it's not cabbages," said Wiley.

"Or cucumbers," I reminded him.

We talked of our travels, possible places, and harvests. Wiley left to find the waiter, leaving us alone. Kate slipped a piece of folded paper into my hand.

"This is my address," she said, looking into my eyes. "I want you to write to me as often as you can. I am going to save the letters in a scrapbook to show the children."

Putting the paper in my pocket and gulped. "Um, children?"

Squeezing my hand, she said softly, "Hopefully our children."

My breath caught in my throat, and my whole being felt like jelly in a bag.

Thankfully Wiley returned at that moment. "Let's go Kate, time for you to board the train home."

At the station, Kate kissed my cheek and winked. "Next time, stop by our house before you go to New York."

"You have my promise," I said, blushing as Kate boarded the train.

Wiley and I went back into the station and asked the clerk for a map of Indiana. At first, he gave us an 'I'm-busy-go-away' look. Suddenly his eyes popped open along with his mouth.

"You're those two guys!"

"Yes we are," I said. "Now we are off on another adventure, if you can find us a map of Indiana." He looked under the counter and came up with a map.

"Can my friend take my picture with you," asked the clerk.

"Yes he can, but please hurry. We may need to leave soon," I told him.

As it turned out, three people got a picture: the clerk, a porter, and the lady from the office who owned the camera. Then, we sat on a bench, spread out the map, and chose Tipton as the destination. "Lots of farms around Tipton," the Porter offered.

Our train left at 2:30 p.m., which gave us half an hour to kill. Walking around the big station, we found a tattoo parlor but decided against getting one. Several shoeshine stands were set up, but our work boots would not take well to polish. Two working girls offered to take us to a nearby hotel for a party. "Thank you for the offer ladies, but our train leaves in fifteen minutes," Wiley said, tipping his hat.

We boarded the train and took a seat. The conductor came around, saw our gold tickets, and said, "Anything you gentlemen wish, just tell the Porter. There is no charge." With a slight jerk, the huge engine began another journey.

I was lost in thoughts of Kate when Wiley asked me, "Your being very quiet. Anything special on your mind?"

I blushed a bit. "Actually, I was thinking about your sister."

Smiling, he asked, "What about Kate?"

"Well, she's very beautiful and she asked me to write to her," I said.

Wiley couldn't hold it any longer. His body was shaking with quiet laughter.

"Don't laugh at me you oaf," I muttered. "I'm really confused right now. I mean, we just met."

"Kate has that effect on people, especially when she plans to marry them."

Sitting up straight, I stared at him. "She told you about that?"

"She asked me endlessly about you," Wiley said, "and, naturally, I told her all I knew." Again with a smile, he said, "Then last night she informed the family she was going to marry you. When Kate makes up her Irish mind, nothing stops her. By the way, I'm to be your best man."

"Does she often plan to marry people she's never met?"

Wiley shook his head. "Never. Guess you're the lucky one."

I questioned Wiley at length about Kate. She was twenty years old, played the violin, and worked in the office of a bank.

"She is a wizard with numbers," Wiley told me, "has been since grade school."

"Does she cook a decent meal?" I asked.

Rolling his eyes, Wiley said, "She took two classes in cooking and one in baking, like pies and pastries."

"She could have any man she wanted," I said. "Why pick me?"

Wiley laughed. "I asked her that very same question. Kate said 'because he touches my heart.' You might as well surrender my Irish friend, your future is now in her hands."

CHAPTER TEN

It was July, with no rain in the forecast and the nights nearly as hot as the days. We found work almost immediately. As we got off the train in Tipton, a local farmer was there picking up a shipment of salt blocks for his cows. Wiley elbowed me in the ribs, nodding toward the man.

"Can we help you with that?" I asked.

Looking at us for a few moments, he nodded. "Sure would be grateful, thanks." When we finished loading the blocks in the back of his old Ford pick-up truck, he asked, "You boys looking for work?"

"We are," said Wiley, "and we both know how to handle a pitchfork."

"I've got maybe three days' work at a dollar a day. Name's Bob Jones." We shook hands and introduced ourselves. "Hop in the back and I'll take you to my farm."

When word got around that two strong boys were willing to help with the hay harvest, the jobs poured in. After Bob's farm, we went to his neighbor David Kliest, then Alfred Metzger. We slept in barns and ate outdoors with the families. After two weeks, we decided to move on. After Mr. Metzger paid us, he mentioned that his brother-in-law, Randall Kroeger, had a big sweet corn farm outside Mt.

Vernon, Ohio. "They're just starting their harvest and are always looking for help." We thanked him and caught a ride back to Tipton.

"Yes the train stops at Mt. Vernon," the ticket clerk said. "Tickets cost $2.50." We showed him our gold tickets, and his brow wrinkled as he frowned.

"Where did you get those?" he asked sharply. I took out the letter that came with the tickets and handed it to him. As he read it, his frown formed into a smile. "Well now, this is a new one on me. I recall reading the story, now here you are." Shaking hands, he told us the train left at seven that evening and that if we needed a good meal, look no further than Pat's Café on Main Street.

As we walked uptown toward the café, I stopped at a Ben Franklin store and bought paper, envelopes, and two pencils. I now had two people to write to.

On the train that evening, I first wrote to Amy and Thomas, telling them where we were and how dry the weather was. I briefly mentioned Kate, saying only that she was Wiley's sister and had asked me to write to her. The letter to Kate was longer. I described the people and the farms, the outdoor meals, and sleeping on fresh hay at night. It seemed vital to get these details down on paper. I closed by saying I'd try to write as often as possible. I would mail the letters at the train station in Mt. Vernon.

At the railroad station, Wiley said, "Let's ask inside where the Post Office is located. They'll know how to get to the farm." The train station clerk motioned over his shoulder with his thumb. "The Post Office is two blocks that way on Maple Street."

An older man, who knew the farm well, sat in the post office behind a half-window wearing rainbow suspenders and a green eyeshade visor.

"Turn right on Maple Street until you hit Fremont Road, then turn left. The farm is seven miles out. You can't miss it."

We thanked him, and I handed him my letters. He nodded, and we headed out the door.

We had gone maybe a mile when an open truck full of corn passed us heading into town. On the side of the truck-box was painted 'Mt. Vernon Cannery'. After another mile, we heard a truck coming up from behind. We waved it down, hoping for a ride.

Through the open passenger window, the driver yelled, "You boys heading to Kroeger's Farm?"

"That we are," I told him. "We're looking for work."

"That's where I'm going. Jump in," he yelled.

The man dropped us off at the gravel drive and then drove out to the cornfield. We walked up to the large two-story white house with blue shutters and a full-length covered front porch. A middle-aged woman came out wiping her hands on an apron.

"You looking for work?" she asked.

"Yes ma'am we are," Wiley told her.

"Randall will be in at noon and I know he can use the help," she said. Looking us over carefully, she smiled. "I'll bet you two haven't eaten today. Hungry?"

"If you can spare a sandwich, that would be fine," I said.

"I can do better than that," she chuckled. She hollered through the screen door, "Betty, fix me two plates!" In minutes another woman appeared carrying plates filled with food. Each plate held a thick pork chop, a long ear of corn, and a biscuit. "Sit here on the porch and eat, I'll get you both a glass of milk."

Randall did hire us. "I've got a month's work for you at a dollar a day. After the corn is picked them stalks get cut down and chopped into silage. There's clean bunks in the barn and you can wash up at the pump."

After we'd dropped our gear in the barn, Randall picked up two odd-looking leather half-gloves from the bed of his truck. In the center of each was a wicked-looking small curved blade. The glove was fastened in the back with a wide leather strap. He handed them to us and showed us how to adjust them. "You keep that strap tight or you'll raise blisters from it rubbing back and forth."

Wiley and I got our first lesson in harvesting sweet corn: grab the ear of corn in one hand, then cut the ear from the stalk with the blade attached to the glove on the other hand. A truck kept pace with us as men on both sides tossed the ears into the truck-bed. Each stalk held several ears, and if you missed one, the guy behind you let you know. "Dammit kid, get them all," I heard a few times.

The trucks left for the cannery at sundown, and we wearily made our way back to the house. Taking off the cutter, I saw I had raised a blister.

One of the older guys, Eddie, said, "We all get them at first. I got some salve at the barn will help."

More corn on the cob with sausage and bread for supper, with plenty of iced tea. Wiley had the same blisters, and Eddie gave us both some magic lotion that soothed the burn. The night was warm with a slight southerly breeze.

"That blister is on the hand you write with," Wiley said with his usual grin, "I hope Kate will be able to read your next letter."

Grinning back, I said, "Kate will be happy to get my letters, so have your fun."

His smirk dissolved, and he nodded. "I think Kate has chosen well."

CHAPTER ELEVEN

Randall Kroeger had three fields of sweet corn to harvest and get to the cannery while the corn was at its peak. We worked six days a week, sun up to sun down. My blisters turned to calluses in time as I learned to get every ear. Then we were done. Nothing but stalks left in the fields. For one day, Randall was happy. Then we started cutting and chopping the stalks into silage to fill the two big silos. This would be fed to the cows during the winter.

The Kroeger's milked twenty Holstein cows daily. This chore was handled by Mrs. Kroeger and their two teenage sons, Clifton, age fourteen, and Howard, sixteen. One early Sunday morning, Clifton offered to teach me how to hand milk a cow. After a few false starts, I finally caught on—another first to tell Kate.

August found us in Illinois, pitchforking second crop hay. Three farms back to back working six days a week. On a Saturday evening, we headed to Minnesota, taking our last ride using our gold tickets. I unlaced my boots and pulled out the money within. I was shocked to find out I had thirty-seven dollars! Wiley had thirty-five. We had the same thought at the same time.

"What now?" I asked.

Wiley said, "First thing, we need new clothes. Ours are used up, and maybe some boots."

I agreed. "Even with a room and meals, we will still have over twenty dollars apiece."

Snapping his fingers, Wiley said, "What we do is get a money order from a bank and send it to Kate. She can bank it for us in Trenton." It was a good plan.

We reached New Ulm, Minnesota just after seven in the evening. We passed a large brown house three blocks from the train station with a sign: ROOMS FOR RENT. I knocked on the door and waited. A bald man wearing glasses opened the door.

"Good evening sir," said Wiley. "We're seeking a room overnight."

"We only rent by the week or month," he said abruptly and closed the door.

We kept walking and eventually reached the downtown area. The New Ulm Hotel was much friendlier.

"We have a room with two single beds for a dollar a night," the clerk said. "The bathroom is at the end of the hall."

"Is there a Catholic Church nearby?" I asked.

"One block over is St. Peter's church with services at seven and ten," he replied.

"You must be planning on attending mass tomorrow," Wiley said as we dropped our bags on the bed.

I sat down. "I'll be writing Kate a letter tomorrow and would like to tell her that 'we' went to church."

Nodding his head, Wiley agreed. "She'll be pleased to know that 'we' did indeed attend the ten o'clock mass."

The following morning, we bathed, shaved, got coffee at a café across the street, and walked to the church. We wore the best clothes we had, threadbare as they were. It was a fine mass with a sermon on helping your fellow man. As we filed out, a well-dressed older couple stopped us.

"We are Adam and June Higgins," the gentleman said. "You young men are new here. Just passing through?"

"We arrived late last night and are looking for work," I answered.

"What kind of work?" Adam asked.

"As you may be able to tell by or clothing, mostly farm work," Wiley said.

"Our church basement is well stocked with clothing donations," said June. "Please, come with us."

Wiley and I were able to stock up on underwear, socks, shirts, pants, hats, and we both found good boots. When we offered to pay, they politely refused to take anything.

"We would like both of you to come to our house for Sunday dinner," said Adam.

When we were down south, Sunday dinner meant chicken. In Minnesota, it was roast beef. During the meal, Adam and June relayed to us a sad and tender story.

"We had a son, Jacob," Adam said, "who joined the Marines during the Great War. He was killed in June 1918 leading a charge at Belleau Wood, that's near the Marne River in France." June showed us a picture of Jacob in his uniform.

"He was only twenty-three years old, and we miss him so," sighed June. "A good boy, hard worker. You both remind us of him, and we'd like to offer any help if we can."

We asked if they knew of any farms hiring workers. "Harold Beckman is putting up his last hay," Adam said and gave us the address, wishing us well.

CHAPTER TWELVE

The Beckman farm lay north of New Ulm along a county road. We got a ride with a delivery man.

Harold was behind in his hay cutting because his tractor had broken down, and he was using two teams of horses to finish up. He offered us three days' work, with lodging in the barn. The harvest went slower, even with our extra hands.

John, one of Harold's regular hands, saw the bright orange glow and dark smoke in the western sky. "Fire! Someone's field is burning!"

"Unhook the horses!" Harold yelled. "Everybody head for the river!" The Minnesota river was a half-mile away. The smoke was getting thicker and darker as the fire moved quickly. When we got to the river, the men and horses never stopped. Instead, we all slid down the sloping brushy bank right into the water. Harold waded out chest-deep and motioned to bring the horses forward. We all followed, stopping about fifteen feet from shore. The heat was intense, and the glowing red embers made an evil hissing sound as they hit the water.

The smoke got so thick I could barely see Wiley standing next to me. Coughing, I felt someone throw a wet neckerchief around my mouth. My eyes burned, and I closed them tightly, thinking of Kate. Only Kate.

Within thirty minutes, the raging fire burned itself out. John and another man climbed up the bank, testing for a path to bring the horses up.

"All you men move forward," Harold ordered. "Make a wide path for the horses. Stomp out any embers so the horses don't burn their feet." We reached a dirt track that led to a county road. We met up with a very surprised fire crew. They handed us cups of water from a barrel, and we all drank like it was going to run out. Thanking the fire crew, we started back to the farm.

The wide county road had saved Harold's farm. Pushed by the westerly wind, the fire swung into the hayfield. Harold's wife was waiting in the yard with tears running down her face as we trudged up the driveway.

"I thought you all had burned," she said, hugging her husband.

"We're fine, dear. Thanks to a great crew," Harold said, "We lost the wagons and the hay-loader but we made it to the river just in time."

We washed off the soot from the horses and then took turns cleaning up at the pump when the sheriff's car, lights flashing, drove up.

"Is everyone alright," he shouted, getting out of the car.

"Calm down Amos, we are all fine," Harold assured him. "Do you know where the fire started?"

"We know it started out at the Bielfuss farm, but we don't yet know how it started," Sheriff Amos said, hands on his hips. "You sure you're okay, Harold?"

"My insurance will cover the wagons and loader, but I may have to buy some hay in the spring." He then told the sheriff about the race to the river, and as he did, it dawned on me how fortunate we had been.

Handing us two dollars each, Harold asked Sheriff Amos if he would give us a ride back to town. On the way into town, the sheriff asked us what our plans were.

"We haven't decided yet," I said. "Do you know of anyone hiring?"

"Not much work around here when the hay crop is in," the Sheriff said, "but my Deputy, Will Haines, just got back from visiting his family in Crawford, Tennessee. He said the pear harvest is starting, also the tomato crop is almost ready."

We talked to Deputy Haines, who informed us that the biggest pear orchard in Tennessee, Farnsworth Farms, is just beginning to harvest the pears. "My cousin Delton Haines works there, just tell him I sent you." We thanked him and walked over to the bus station.

"Tickets to Crawford, one way, two dollars each," said the clerk. Smiling and laughing, we bought the tickets.

The clerk frowned, "What's so damn funny?"

"You must pardon us," Wiley said, "On our only job here, we made just enough money to leave town." It was four o'clock and the bus left at six that evening. We returned to the hotel, checked out, and found a café. Meatloaf, mashed potatoes, and coffee would have to do until we got to Tennessee.

With several hours to kill, I took out paper and pencil and began a letter to Kate.

"Are you going to tell her about the fire?" Wiley asked.

"I have to," I told him. "Keeping secrets is no way to start a true relationship."

Wiley had relaxed with his hat pulled down over his face, but I could still see the smile. "It is a fine husband you will make for my baby sister," he said softly, then drifted off to sleep.

The letter was three pages long, telling all that had happened. I said I missed Kate's lovely smile and wished to see her soon. I enclosed the fifty-dollar money order from the New Ulm Bank and sealed it, intending to mail it from Crawford, Tennessee.

CHAPTER THIRTEEN

Farnsworth Farms was indeed hiring. Walter and Ellen Farnsworth, along with two sons, Allen and Leon, ran the operation. "Pick out a cot in the men's tent and I'll get you started," Allen said. The tents, the blankets, and the folding cots were U.S. Army surplus, with the musty smell of storage. I noticed two shower stations with wooden floors and overhead tanks behind the tent. Allen took our names and directed us to a pile of small sacks with long straps.

"The strap goes over your shoulder. The pears go into the sack. When the sack is full, dump it into one of the baskets." I wondered how many times Allen had given this speech.

His brother Leon ran our work crew. The women picked the lower branches while men with ladders got the higher pears. Two trucks worked the field, picking up the full baskets, stacking them four high on the truck-bed. On the side of the trucks was the sign 'Blue Star Cannery.'

The food was good, if predictable. This evening it was a beef stew with bread and more tea. I was learning that tea replenishes much-needed nutrients the body sweats out under the hot sun. We met Delton Haines, who resembled his cousin, Will, coming in from the orchard. We told him about the fire and our close call.

"This damn drought has everything tinder dry," Delton said. "Allen won't let anyone smoke on the property. You have to walk out to the county road."

There were three orchards to pick, which took us three weeks. When we finished on a Friday afternoon, they set up the payment table in the yard with Walter and Ellen handing out the money. Allen stood to one side, talking to certain workers as they passed. He beckoned to Wiley and me.

"We have one-hundred-fifty acres of tomatoes that need picking. Interested?"

"Yes we are," answered Wiley, "and thank God it's not cabbages."

Laughing, Allen said, "Take the weekend off. We start picking Monday morning."

"You have to be gentler with the tomatoes," Leon instructed. "Don't throw them in the baskets, set them in." We soon found out why. Some tomatoes are riper than others. Again the cannery trucks picked up the baskets, this time laying boards across each tier, stacking only three high.

Many calloused hands emptied the tomato field in a week. After drawing our pay, we asked Allen if any other people were hiring nearby. "Matt Crosley has a big apple orchard. His place is just down the road eight miles. He should be hiring about now."

Mr. Crosley was hiring. This time we would be sleeping in the barn. The picking was much the same as pears. We greeted some familiar faces, one of them Delton Haines. Also familiar was Loretta, the sixteen-year-old daughter of Jake and Estelle Burnett. Loretta was developed beyond her age and had an eye for Wiley. Estelle noticed but did or said nothing. Jake paid no attention; he just kept picking apples.

That evening after supper, Wiley and I walked out to the gravel drive so he could have his occasional cigarette.

"Young Loretta has designs on you," I told him.

"I have noticed," Wiley said, "and, although she is available, I don't wish for her to bear my children."

That night we decided to sleep in the orchard rather than the tent. Just after midnight, we heard shouting coming from the men's tent. Creeping closer, we saw it all unfold. "Hey! What the hell are you doing! Get out of here!" The yard light came on in time for all to see Loretta come running from the men's tent. Standing right outside was her mother, Estelle.

"Wiley Bishop, you get out here!" she demanded. An older man with a paunch and wearing glasses emerged.

"That little slut tried to get in my cot!" he yelled. Allen came from the house, asking what was going on. Sensing a big mistake had been made, Estelle covered up well.

"It's so dark, my daughter entered the wrong tent by mistake. Are you alright dear?" Sniffling, Loretta nodded her head and returned to the women's tent with her mother's arm around her. Grumbling, Allen returned to the house, and the yard light went out. Running back into the orchard so no one would hear us, Wiley and I laughed until we collapsed.

It was September now. The nights were a bit cooler but still no rain in the forecast. The apple crop was in, the workers paid, and we were on our way back to Crawford. It was Saturday morning, so we had no problem getting a ride. We got a room at the Crawford Hotel for a dollar a night. After a hot bath, a shave, and a change of clothes, we walked to the barbershop for a much-needed haircut. Wiley went first while I read the latest newspaper. On the front page was a story about a brewery in town being torn down. I asked the old barber about it.

"That old brewery was just fine until some hobos passing through started a cooking fire that got out of control," he snorted.

"Are they hiring any help?" I asked.

"Oh sure," he replied, "if you can handle a wheelbarrow and a shovel, the town is paying a dollar a day."

CHAPTER FOURTEEN

We worked at the old brewery for a week. The fire had ravaged the entire building. The heat warped the brewing tanks, and much of the equipment had melted. The big stuff, like beams and doors, we carried to the waiting trucks. The rest, we shoveled into wheelbarrows. The town provided sandwiches for lunch with, of course, more tea. By the end of the week, Wiley and I realized we were barely breaking even. Paying for the room and supper left us with no money saved. We quit that Friday afternoon, packed our bags, and left town. This time we decided to thumb a ride.

"Let's try Virginia," I said. "The apple crops should be ready."

"Better apples than tomatoes," said Wiley. We got a ride within fifteen minutes from a salesman with the McCormick-Deering Company.

"I'm going to Murfreesboro," he told us, "The company is setting up a farm implement dealership there."

"How do you sell tractors and equipment with the whole country in a depression," I asked him.

"The federal Government is helping the bigger farms with loans," he said. "They realize the nation has to eat, no matter what." He took us to the east side of town and let us out. We walked about a mile, talking of work, the drought, and possibly going home for a visit.

The sun was a burning red ball slowly sinking in the west when we heard the auto behind us. It came to a gentle rumbling stop next to us. The young man behind the wheel was smiling when he asked if we needed a ride.

"I'm going to Crossville," he said. Without a thought, Wiley got in the back, and I settled in the front. Holding out his hand, the man said, "I'm Dooley Barnes."

We shook hands, and Wiley asked, "This is a nice auto. Who makes it?"

"It's a 1927 REO," Dooley said proudly. "It's got a V-8 engine, a really great suspension, new tires and good brakes." I looked over at the speedometer and saw we were going 70 mph. I looked back at Wiley and saw his face go a little pale.

"We are going quite fast," I said to Dooley.

"Yes we are," Dooley said with a smile. "In a few minutes you will see why."

As we sailed over a small hill, I heard Dooley mutter to himself. "They should be right around this curve." The auto held the road as Dooley took the curve at 70 mph. We sped past two vehicles parked beside the highway, who pulled out and fell in behind us. The auto directly behind us turned on its lights and siren. The auto directly behind us turned on its lights and siren. Dooley was laughing now and held his speed.

Wiley's voice held a higher pitch when he asked, "Aren't you going to pull over?"

"Oh no," Dooley said. "I want them to chase me."

I couldn't believe what I was hearing! "Why do you want them chasing you?"

Still smiling, Dooley explained. "You see fellas, this is what we call the chase car. That state cop behind me and the revenuers in the car behind him think I'm hauling moonshine." I was sure I could hear Wiley praying in the backseat.

"Are you hauling moonshine?" I asked shakily.

Laughing now, Dooley said, "No moonshine in this car, but the car two miles behind this little parade is making a run to Chicago with a full load. My job is to make the cops chase me instead of the real 'shine hauler."

At times the speed got up to 80 mph. When the police car fell too far behind, Dooley would slow down to let him catch up. The big REO held the road like it was on a rail. Hills, long curves, passing vehicles, Dooley drove like a professional race car driver. He was completely at ease as we screamed down the highway.

"What happens when we get to Crossville?" I asked.

"That's the end of my chase," Dooley said, "I pull over in front of the police station and let them arrest me." Wiley slowly sank back into the seat. I thought he had passed out, but he was still praying.

"Will they arrest us too?" I asked Dooley.

"I'll tell them I gave you two a ride, and they'll let you go on your way," he said.

Dooley rolled to a stop in front of the Crossville Police Station. Minutes later, the cars chasing them drove up. The state patrolman turned off the lights and siren, stepped out of his car, and walked over.

"Get out of the car, all three of you," he demanded. The police patted us down for any firearms. Then a Federal agent walked up.

Pointing at the police officer, he ordered, "Take this car apart, I want that illegal liquor." And that is what they did.

The backseat was pulled out; the trunk was searched, two police crawled under the REO looking for moonshine. The state trooper gently placed his hand on Dooley's shoulder.

"You were the chase car, weren't you?" he asked.

Still smiling, Dooley replied, "I don't know what you're talking about, sir. I was just giving these two boys a ride to town so they wouldn't miss their bus."

Turning toward Wiley and me, the trooper sighed, "Get your bags and beat it." We did.

CHAPTER FIFTEEN

Tickets to Farmville, Virginia were two dollars each. We gladly paid. Even though the bus didn't leave for an hour, we waited at the station where it was quiet, and there were no police.

"We could have been killed," Wiley kept saying.

"I don't believe we were ever in any danger," I said. "Dooley was in total control of that car."

"What if that cop had started shooting at us," Wiley whispered forcefully. As he continued his tirade, I sat back and listened, nodding my head now and then. Eventually, Wiley wound down.

"Why are we going to Farmville?" he asked.

After an earful of panic and calamity, his change in thought nearly made me laugh.

I took him over to the map on the wall and pointed. "From here to there is the Appalachian Mountains. The farms will be on the flatlands, by Farmville."

I would have loved to see the mountains in daylight. As the bus made its way along the winding mountain road, I could feel the hills, the valleys, the curves, and the sharp bends in the road. In the distance, an occasional faint glow from a faraway house. It was too dark to write a letter or read my small Bible, so my thoughts naturally focused on Kate. The picture of her in my mind was sharp and clear, never blurred nor fading. I knew I must see her soon. We had much to talk about and much planning to do.

When I awoke, the dark gray sky held a fringe of pale yellow. I poked Wiley in the ribs.

"Time to wake up, we should be in Farmville soon." Lifting the hat, he glanced out the bus window. Sitting up, he yawned and rubbed his face with both hands.

"If I don't eat soon I may pass away," he grumbled.

The Valley Café was a half-block from the bus station. Someone had left a copy of the local Farmville newspaper on the seat of the booth we chose. As coffee and pancakes filled our empty bellies, I read the paper. Thackery Orchards was looking for pickers. As the waitress walked over to fill our coffee cups (the first refill was free), I asked her about Thackery Orchards.

"You looking for work?" she asked.

"Indeed we are," Wiley spoke up, "and we have experience."

Looking toward one of the customers at the counter, she called, "Hey Ben, got two pickers for you."

A tall thin man looked over and raised his hand. "Be right with you," he called back.

Ben Thackery had two hundred acres of apples to get to the Farmville cannery. We followed him out to his flatbed truck, got in, and off we went.

Another set of Army tents with folding cots was waiting for us. Dumping our bags on two empty cots, we followed Ben into the orchard. Wiley and I each picked up a bag from a pile, slung them over our shoulders, and started picking. There were several women pickers, but we didn't see Loretta or her mother. A truck drove slowly down the access lane, stopped, and began loading the baskets of apples. The sun was hot, and we worked up a good sweat before lunch.

An old brown driver, with an old brown horse pulling a small wagon, brought out our lunch—bologna and cheese sandwiches and a big can of cold water with a dipper hanging on the side. We ate sitting under a tree with a middle-aged man named Clyde.

"Me and my wife Doris have been following the harvest for two years now," Clyde told us. "Ain't much about apples we don't know."

"Is there another farm after this?" I asked him.

"Taylor's Orchard on the other side of Farmville," said Clyde. We finished the sandwiches and went back to work.

It took two weeks to empty the trees in Ben's orchard. We finished on a Friday at noon. As we all walked into the yard, we were greeted with sawhorses and board tables loaded down with food. Ben's wife, Ginny, had been busy laying out a feast for the pickers. Chicken, potato salad, sliced tomatoes, rolls, and pitchers of iced tea. Wiley and I sat down to eat with Clyde and Doris.

"I think Wiley and I will go to that Taylor's Orchard you told us about," I said.

"You can ride in the back of our pick-up truck," Doris said. "It's not that far, but it's too hot to walk. We leave tomorrow morning."

I wrote Kate another letter that night telling her where we were going. Wiley and I had decided to work our way back to New Jersey. Soon the squash and pumpkin harvest would begin. I also remembered Emmett Castle and his potatoes and carrots I had helped plant. They should almost be ready to harvest. Wiley was talking to two other men about possible work. It was late September, and the apple harvest was almost done. Now the garden crops were ready to dig up. Time to get our hands dirty.

CHAPTER SIXTEEN

Taylor's Orchards were already half-picked when we arrived Saturday morning. Anson Taylor took our names, saying, "Grab a sack, start picking, the trucks are on the way." Leaving our things on Clyde's truck, we walked out in the orchard. Men picked from ladders while the women picked the lower branches. The day was cooler, with a hint of darker clouds on the horizon. Everyone prayed for rain.

We slept in the old barn on hastily built bunks, having a supper of sandwiches and watery bean soup. Definitely not a class-A operation. Taylor had one hundred acres to be picked, with the orchard already half done. By the following Tuesday, we were finished.

Wiley and I caught a ride back to Farmville and had supper at the Valley Café. The waitress, Callie, remembered us.

"Picking all done?" she asked.

"We picked every apple. Now we need more work," Wiley said as Callie took our order for roast beef, mashed potatoes, and green beans.

"My ex-husband's family owns the Bascom Produce Farm south of here in Five Forks," Callie said. "Clem was a lazy redneck, but his folks are good people. They are harvesting squash and beets this week. Tell them I sent you."

After supper, Wiley and I walked out to Highway 15 south and stuck out our thumbs. An older couple in a Model-A Ford gave us a ride. When we told them where we were headed, the woman told us, "We go right by the Bascom place." It was dusk when we arrived at the farm.

We walked up the driveway to a white farmhouse. I knocked on the door, and a heavy-set man with gray hair answered.

"You looking for work?" he asked.

"Yes sir we are," I said. "Callie at the Farmville Café sent us."

With a smile, he told us, "If Callie vouches for you, I'll take you on. Have you eaten tonight?" We told him we had. "Find a bunk in the barn, I'll get your names tomorrow."

In the morning, Buford and Eunice Bascom had pots of hot coffee set out for their workers. He wrote down our names in a notebook and said, "You two will be hauling squash today. You bring them to the end of row where a truck will pick them up." He handed us each a pair of leather gloves then pointed the way to the field.

These were Hubbard squash, weighing between fifteen and twenty pounds each. Several women were at work cutting the squash from the vine. Wiley and I each had a wheelbarrow. When the wheelbarrow was loaded, we took them to the end of the row, unloaded, and went back for more.

The morning had been cool, but by noon the sun was blazing. Ginny Bascom bought out sandwiches and a lot of cold tea for lunch. About two o'clock, a flatbed truck with board sides showed up with four men. Two men on the ground tossed up the squash while two men in the truck stacked them. Looking out across the long and wide field, I figured there was at least a week worth of work.

After a beef stew supper, Wiley and I took stock of our situation. As we talked, another man approached.

"I'm Nick Grundy from Ohio," he said. "Where are you guys from?" We told him, and he said, "You got plans after this?"

"We are going to work our way back toward New Jersey," said Wiley. Nick was a few years younger than us, maybe twenty years old, blonde hair with a wispy beard. His brown eyes looked all around as he spoke, and his nervous body movements made me think of someone hiding out or on the run. Wiley sensed it too. Looking at me, he gave a slight 'no' shake of his head. After a while, Nick moved on.

"I wonder who is chasing him," Wiley asked. We found out the next day.

We were having our coffee at sunrise when a police car drove in. Nick quietly set down his cup and faded into the background. Two deputies approached Buford and showed him a picture. "Have you seen this man?" they asked.

Then one of the women pointed and shouted, "There goes Nick! He's running away!" Legs flying and arms pumping, Nick was running across the beet field at full speed. The deputies ran back to their car and sped off. We soon lost sight of Nick and the police car.

That evening we learned what happened. Nick and two friends had robbed a bank in Friendship, Ohio, taking a teller hostage. They held him on the running board of the car as they sped away. A wild shot from a policeman wounded the teller in the leg, and he fell from the getaway car. While being cared for in the local hospital, the teller identified one of the robbers as a local man named Hamilton Lepage. They arrested Hamilton the next day, trying to board a train to Florida. He gave up his two friends, George Cohen and Nick Grundy. George was still at large.

CHAPTER SEVENTEEN

Buford and Ginny Bascom paid us in full on a Saturday morning. "If you're looking for more work, my cousin Elmer Behling has his harvest going. He lives by Warrenton. Tell him I sent you," Buford said.

One of the cannery truck drivers gave us a ride into town. We took a room at the Farmville Hotel, which cost us a dollar, then we bathed, shaved, and changed clothes. I asked the desk clerk about a used clothing store.

"No store," the clerk said, "but the Methodist church has a basement full of old clothes they give away. It's over one block on Chestnut Street." Wiley and I went through our worn clothes. After throwing away what could not be saved, there wasn't much left.

Two ladies were replacing candles on the altar when we entered the church.

"Pardon us ladies," I said. "My friend and I need some clothing. Can you help us?" They took us down some creaky steps to a dimly lit basement. Several tables held what we needed: pants, shirts, socks, and some fall jackets. A rack on the wall had hats and belts. The ladies talked endlessly, asking about our work, and both gave the Bascom's high praise as good people. They turned down our offer to pay for the clothes. Thanking them, we left.

Wiley had got a hat, a gray Fedora, almost new. He kept adjusting it on his head.

"Need another haircut?" I asked. Taking the hat off, he flipped down the sweatband, and out fell a folded five-dollar bill! I grabbed it before it hit the ground.

"That's why it didn't fit right on one side," Wiley said. I handed him the bill. He smiled. "This will pay for our weekend. Let's go to a movie."

Hoot Gibson starred in *King of the Rodeo* at the Metropole movie house. Lots of action. Daring chases on horseback, bucking broncos, lots of shooting, and pretty girls. After the show, we walked toward the café, stopping at a dime store, and bought new underwear and gloves.

At the Valley Café, the special was meatballs and gravy over mashed potatoes with creamed corn and a dinner roll washed down with hot coffee. Back at the hotel, we settled in for the night. I would write Kate tomorrow.

Sunday found us on our way to Warrenton by bus. The weather turned cooler, and we were glad we had found jackets to wear. Leaves were turning to fall colors, and in a few weeks, the state of Virginia would transform into a landscape of red and gold. Harvest time in the east.

"You men are just what I need," said Elmer. "The potatoes come in from the field in baskets and get loaded into one hundred pound sacks." Writing down our names, he said, "Any damaged spuds toss to the side. When the bag is full, tie it off and stack it for pick-up later." I didn't ask how many acres of potatoes he had but knew that and large produce farm would grow at least two hundred acres. Looking at Wiley, I shrugged my shoulders, pulled an empty sack from the pile, and started filling it. Wiley did the same. Four other men were already at work.

Hour after hour, basket after basket, the potatoes kept coming in from the field. An hour after lunch, a flatbed truck drove in with two men in the cab, and two more rode in the back. Without a word, they loaded the potatoes. Two would grab a sack at each end and hoist it to the bed, while the two on the truck then stacked them four bags high. With a full load, the truck left for Warrenton. Still, the baskets kept coming.

With six of us working, we barely managed to keep up. Finally, at sundown, the last baskets were delivered. Around us were several baskets of damaged potatoes that the digger had sliced into or partially crushed. Another worker, Fred, told us, "Those damaged ones Elmer sells to a local pig farmer. He will pick them up tonight."

Supper was another beef stew with *lots* of potatoes. "Fred says there are extra blankets in the barn if it gets cold tonight," Wiley said.

On our way back to the barn, an old Ford pickup truck drove up. The overweight bald man in the cab yelled, "Hey you guys, load them baskets of busted spuds in my truck."

"We charge a nickel a basket," Wiley said with a big grin. Frowning, the man mumbled something about 'cheap labor' then got out and loaded the baskets himself. He did not wave as he drove away.

It took two weeks to bag all the potatoes. When Elmer came around with our pay on Friday, he said, "I'm starting

the beet harvest on Monday, if you men want more work."
We said we would but wanted to go into Warrenton for the
weekend and promised to return Sunday evening.

CHAPTER EIGHTEEN

We got a ride into town Saturday morning with Elmer's foreman, Eugene. Wiley and I had counted our money the night before and decided to send a forty-dollar money order to Kate. That left us nine dollars apiece to spend.

"Let's stop at the bank first," I told Wiley, "then I can send it with the letter I'll write tonight." I stood by the lobby window in the bank, watching the street as Wiley went to the teller with the money. Suddenly, a man and woman burst through the door waving pistols and yelling.

"Everybody, get your hands in the air! This is a holdup! Nobody move!" It was like a moment frozen in time. Along with the two tellers, Wiley, a young couple, an older man, and I were the only customers in the bank. The robber grabbed Wiley by the collar and yanked him down to the floor.

"Stay down kid," he snarled. The woman pointed her pistol at the young couple and the older man, not noticing me by the window. The robber pulled a cloth bag from his shirt, throwing it to the first teller.

"Fill that bag with cash!" He should have been paying attention to Wiley.

It was the first time I had seen Wiley get angry. His face got red as he gritted his teeth. Then he kicked the robber in the back of a knee. With a cry of pain, the robber hit the floor, and Wiley jumped on him! The hand with the pistol was pinned under Wiley's knee as they struggled.

The woman stood with her back toward me with the pistol pointed in the air, not sure what to do. I slipped up quietly behind her, grabbed the gun with my right hand, and circled her waist with my left. Meanwhile, Wiley punched the other robber in the face until the man finally released the weapon, which Wiley snatched up. The two tellers were still standing there with their hands in the air!

"Call the police," I hollered, and one of the tellers ran for the manager's office.

Within minutes, three police rushed through the door, taking the robbers into custody. The teller had also called the bank manager, who arrived in pants, an undershirt, and slippers. Wiley and I stood to one side as an officer took our statements. A reporter and photographer from the newspaper arrived, along with the Mayor and Police Chief. The bank manager, seeing the press, quietly snuck away, ran home and returned fully dressed in suit and tie.

We told the reporter, the bank manager, the Mayor, and the Police Chief our story of who we were and why we were in the bank.

In a moment of weakness, the bank manager exclaimed, "The bank would like to offer a reward of one-hundred dollars for the capture of the robbers!"

Not to be outdone, the Mayor added, "And the town will match that reward!"

Before they could change their minds, Wiley asked the bank teller, "May we add that to our money order?"

Upon approval of the Mayor and bank manager, the teller drafted an order for $240 and handed it to me. I asked the reporter if he would send a copy of the story to Kate and Amy and gave him the addresses. The Police Chief offered to put us up at the hotel in case they needed any more information.

As we walked toward our lodgings, I told Wiley, "We really have to stop doing this before we become famous."

"Perhaps, but it certainly pays better than sacking potatoes," Wiley laughed.

After a hot bath, a shave, and clean clothes, I sat down and wrote to Kate. I explained what had happened, giving most of the credit to Wiley. I told her to expect the newspaper story and enclosed the money order. The desk clerk said he would include it in their outgoing mail.

As we entered the café, someone shouted, "It's them! It's the fellas who stopped the bank robbery!" We shook hands all around, got slapped on the back, and then ushered to a booth by the waitress.

The café owner, Ernie, came out and said, "It'll be my pleasure to serve you men whatever you would like, on the house." We ordered steak, baked potatoes, green beans, and coffee with cherry pie for dessert.

Afterward, we went to the Majestic movie house and saw *All Quiet on the Western Front*. On the way back to the hotel, I asked, "Will you be coming to mass with me tomorrow morning?"

"I will," he said, "to ask forgiveness for losing my Irish temper."

We attended mass at Saint Andrews Church at ten o'clock. Parishioners who had been in the café recognized us, smiled, and waved. After mass, several people invited us for dinner, but the pastor, Father Joseph, said, "I'd like these two young men to dine with me today."

His housekeeper must have suspected that we would be there, as the table she set the table for three. Then she served a delicious roast chicken with dressing and all the trimmings. As we ate, Father Joseph asked for our background. We told him our story, leaving very little out. We left with his blessing and decided to thumb a ride back to Elmer's, accepting a ride from a young couple our for a Sunday drive.

Elmer Behling and his wife Joan must have heard about our bank adventure. As we walked up the drive, they walked down from the house to meet us. "Please come in for a cup of coffee," Joan offered.

"Every dollar we have is in that bank," Elmer said, "you saved or business." Wiley and I tried to explain that we had just been in the wrong place at the right time. We thanked them for the coffee and walked to the barn—time to get some rest.

Harvesting beets was just like harvesting potatoes. Weed out the bad ones, bag the good ones in 100-pound sacks. Stack the bags for pick up by the wholesaler. Wiley and I got joked with by the other men, but it was all good-natured banter. The pig farmer showed up to pick up the culls. He didn't ask for help this time, just frowned, grumbled, and loaded them himself. Two weeks later, and the job was done. Elmer paid us, shook our hands, and had Eugene drive us into town.

CHAPTER NINETEEN

"Let's make one more stop in Plum Pennsylvania," I said, "then we should head home for a visit."

"I'm sure Kate will be glad to see us both." Wiley smiled.

At the bus station, we checked the map on the wall. It would be a long trip to Plum, with many stops in between. Tickets were $2.75 each, the bus leaving at two in the afternoon. We just had time for lunch.

It was October now. The nights were chilly, the days bearable. Except for the deep south, the harvest was almost over. Emmett Castle should have about a week's work for us, then Wiley and I would be on our way to Trenton, New Jersey. Thoughts of Kate filled my head. It still amazed me that this lovely young woman had picked me. I looked over at Wiley, asleep with his hat pulled down over his eyes. I had never known a closer friendship or trusted another person like I did Wiley. I said a silent prayer of thanks and drifted off to sleep.

Emmett Castle was glad to see us. "I had two men quit on me yesterday, said the work was too hard." Emmett was doing what we had already done—sorting through the baskets of potatoes, weeding out the culls, and bagging them in 100-pound sacks. Wiley and I went right to work. Two other men were doing the same. By evening we had caught up. We had dropped our bags in the barn and noticed a wood stove was going with the smoke piped out through the side of the barn. A pile of split wood sat just inside the door. One of the other men, Donald, told us, "We take turns at night keeping the fire going. It don't look like much, but it keeps us warm."

The carrots started coming in right on the heels of the potatoes. They were a little easier because the carrots were bagged in fifty-pound sacks. The same wholesaler who bought the potatoes also got the carrots. In ten days, the job was done.

As Emmett paid us, he said, "I hope to see you men in the spring for planting time." One of the truckers gave us a ride into Plum.

We decided to travel to Trenton by train, but the nearest station was in Pittsburgh. A short bus ride landed us at the Pittsburgh Railway station. The train to Trenton cost two dollars each. It was eleven in the morning, three hours before our train left.

"Let's get cleaned up and get a meal," I said.

"Don't we have to get a room to get a bath for that?" Wiley asked. We found a run-down hotel two blocks away. With a folded dollar bill between my fingers, I told the desk clerk, "My friend and I need to take a bath and change clothes."

The dollar went from my hand to his pocket as he said, "Don't take all damn day."

Joe's Diner was serving meatloaf, mashed potatoes, and gravy. The stout gray-haired waitress asked if we wanted dessert. "We have apple pie, with a scoop of ice cream," she said. We each took a large slice.

As she refilled our coffee, she said, "You boys must be waiting for the train."

"We're going home to Trenton," Wiley said. We paid for the meal and walked back to the station.

The Pullman car was warm and comfortable as we settled in for the long ride across Pennsylvania. "How far to Trenton, New Jersey?" I asked the conductor.

"As the crow flies, 325 miles," he said. "By rail, it's 350."

"Any stops?" I asked.

"Three stops along the way. We should be in Trenton by nine o'clock tonight."

Wiley was already slouched down in the window seat, relaxing. "How far from the station to your house?" I asked.

With his usual grin, he replied, "Three blocks, and yes, Kate will be home."

Knowing there was no way I would get any sleep, I took out my pocket Bible and randomly chose a page. I read for maybe ten minutes, but Kate occupied my mind. Had time and distance changed her mind? Did she think of me as often as I thought of her? Did she still wish to marry me? I had never had a steady girlfriend, just a few dates with local girls from the Bronx. None of them compared to Kate, not even close.

I awoke with Wiley poking me in the side. "Let's go to the club car. Maybe they got some coffee." The club car was two cars ahead.

As we entered, a Porter asked, "What can I get you gentlemen?"

"Some hot coffee would be nice," I said. He returned with the coffee and a napkin-covered plate.

"Fresh cinnamon rolls right from the oven," he said with a smile.

This is the kind of train travel I like.

CHAPTER TWENTY

Stepping down from the train in Trenton, we pushed our way through the crowd and emerged on the street. "The house is three blocks that way, "Wiley said, pointing to his right. "My sister Mattie is married to a fireman named Sean Flanagan, another fine son of the old Sod."

"How old are the nephews," I asked.

"Patrick is seven, in second grade," said Wiley, "and Liam is five. This is his first year in kindergarten."

"Are you sure it'll be alright with them if we just drop in?"

Laughing, Wiley said, "By now, Kate has already firmly set your place in the family."

We arrived at the Flanagan home on Hudson Street. Wiley knocked loudly, then opened the door and entered with me right behind.

"It's Uncle Wiley!" The older boy, Patrick, threw his arms around Wiley's legs.

"Uncle Wiley!" A younger boy, Liam, did the same.

Sean Flanagan came from the kitchen laughing. "By the saints, you made it home again," he said, giving Wiley a hug. His sister Mattie was dusting her hands on her apron as she came raced to greet us.

"God saw you safely home," she sighed with tears in the corners of her eyes as she hugged Wiley. Then they noticed me.

"You're Danny Broome," Sean said firmly, shaking my hand.

Mattie hugged me, saying, "Welcome to our family." Standing in the doorway of the kitchen was Kate. The kitchen light behind her gave her the aura of an angel. Noticing her, the family parted, and she walked straight to my arms. For the first time, we kissed. It was a soft, sweet moment for both of us. We parted, and she gave Wiley a hug and kiss on the cheek.

Mattie broke the silence. "There's hot coffee on and rolls fresh from the oven. Come and sit down."

They all wanted to know about the bank robbery. "As a boy, he was always fighting," Mattie said, "but as he got older he grew out of it."

"I won half and lost half, so I quit when I broke even," Wiley said, laughing. They asked about my family, and I told them about my sister Amy and her husband, Thomas.

"I will see them on Sunday, if Kate would like to go with me," I said, looking at her.

"I gladly will," she said. "It will give us time to talk of the future."

The boys had school in the morning and were sent off to bed. Wiley and I slept on the living room floor, exhausted from the journey and the welcome home.

I woke early to the sounds of boys getting ready for school. I was not truly sure of the day but felt it might be Friday. The soft whirring of a treadle sewing machine and the smell of hot coffee let me know I would not be getting back to sleep. I dressed and walked to the kitchen. Kate was dishing up oatmeal for the boys as I sat down at the kitchen table. Without a word, a cup of coffee appeared before me.

"Good morning Danny," she said, kissing me softly on my cheek.

Patrick had been watching as he ate and asked, "Are you going to be living here with us?"

"That would be an unnecessary burden on the family," I said, "so I will be finding my own place."

"Will you still come to visit?" said Liam, looking sad.

Smiling, I replied, "I will visit as often as your Aunt Kate will allow."

"And that may be quite often," added Kate. A horn sounded outside. As the boys scrambled from the table, Kate yelled, "Coats, mittens, hats and books!" Within minutes the door slammed, and the silence was broken only by the sound of the sewing machine. Without waiting for a question, Kate said, "Mattie is something of a seamstress. At present she is altering some church vestments."

Kate poured herself a coffee and sat down. "I have done some checking and I believe I have a solution to yours and Wiley's living arrangements. Six blocks from here is a YMCA. The membership is five dollars per month and you both will eat meals here."

"You are the most organized person I have ever met," I said. "How do you do it?"

Blushing a bit, Kate answered, "For every problem there is a solution. Planning ahead is what keeps the wolf from the door."

"Before we get too far into the future, there is something I must ask you," I told her. I rose from the table and got down on one knee. Taking both her hands in mine, I asked softly, "Will you Kate Bishop, take in marriage this poor lovesick Irishman Danny Broome?"

Smiling, with tears in her eyes, Kate replied, "I have been waiting for you since before we met. It will be my dream come true to be your wife." She rose slowly from her chair, and our arms encircled each other as our lips met. We were lost in the moment, our first real lover's embrace.

"As soon as you two are finished, I could really use some coffee." Wiley stood in the kitchen doorway smiling, and right behind him was Mattie sniffling into a handkerchief. A little embarrassed but happy, we all broke into laughter.

Mattie came forward to hug us. "I am so happy for both of you," she said, "and I am not sure how, but I am sure God had a hand it this somewhere."

CHAPTER TWENTY-ONE

After breakfast, Kate left for work at the bank while Wiley and I rode the bus to the YMCA. It was an old six-story hotel that had been remodeled. An older man introduced himself as Tyler Holdren. "Fill out these membership cards and come to my office when you have finished," he said.

Tyler had us both take a chair. "I am in need of a physical Education instructor," he said, "and both of you seem quite physically fit. Take a minute and decide between yourselves who most needs the work." Placing his elbows on his desk, he continued. "The classes are two hours long, five days a week from two until four every afternoon, and pays two dollars per class. The membership would be free."

Wiley spoke up. "It is a fine offer sir, but as an instructor I would be less than effective. My friend Danny is your obvious choice." We shook hands on the deal, and the clerk showed us to our rooms. They were tastefully done, each with its own bathroom. "Another feather in Kate's cap," Wiley said with a grin.

As we left, Wiley said, "Kate mentioned that the Roosevelt Elementary School near the bank where she works is looking for a janitor. Let's take a look." The city bus dropped us by the school. We walked in, unsure of what to expect. We found the main office at the end of the hall and entered.

A dark-haired woman behind the counter frowned and asked, "To what do I owe the pleasure of your visit?"

Wiley put on his best smile. "My sister, Kate Bishop, said you may need a janitor."

The frown was replaced with a smile. "Would you happen to be her brother, Wiley?"

"I am that, and you must be Anne Southerby, the principal. You're just as Kate described you."

"Kate and I try to have lunch together as often as possible. A lovely young woman, and a dear friend," Anne said. She showed us around the school. "I had to fire the last janitor for theft. He was stealing the cleaning supplies and selling them cheap to restaurants."

"What are the hours?" Wiley asked.

"You would be cleaning Monday through Friday afternoons from three until six. The pay is a dollar per hour."

"I can start Monday," Wiley told her, "and thank you for the opportunity."

By three that afternoon, Wiley and I were back home with Mattie. "If we are going to be eating here," I said, "then Wiley and I should be helping. Make a shopping list and we will fill it." Mattie grabbed a piece of paper and a pencil and began jotting down items. Now and then, she would open and close cupboard doors, checking stock.

"It's vegetable soup tonight," she said, "but Sunday it's corned beef and cabbage, Sean's favorite." Wiley and I walked to the market a block and a half away. The order filled four bags, and we felt like kings returning home with food. Kate arrived as we were unpacking in the kitchen.

"We are celebrating a most productive day," I told her.

"And what trouble did you two manage to get into?" she asked. Wiley was in his glory telling about our employment and the rooms at the YMCA. Kate was beaming as we laid the credit for it all on her lovely shoulders. "I will make a special dessert tomorrow," she said. "It will be a grand evening."

Sean and the two boys arrived about the same time. Hearing the news, he said, "I take it you both will be around for the Holidays." Looking at each other, we realized we'd be spending Thanksgiving and Christmas at home, not on the road.

Saturday was laundry day. As I unpacked my clothing, Kate was looking over my shoulder. "You have one shirt and one pair of pants that are fit to wear, and you are wearing them. Throw the rest in the trash. We are going shopping." Wiley got much the same treatment from Mattie.

"I will not wash rags," she said, "now go get some decent clothes."

Stopping at the bank, Wiley and I both withdrew twenty dollars from the savings account Kate had set up for us. "There is a sale on men's clothing at Piper's Department Store," Kate said. "Nothing fancy, just good quality clothing." Again, she was right. It was over a year since I had bought anything to wear that was new—two pairs of pants, three shirts, underwear, socks, gloves, and new boots.

"You will both need a heavier coat for winter," Kate explained. Added up, the total cost was $17.50 apiece. Every purchase met with Kate's approval. Kissing my cheek, she said, "Now we can be seen together in public, with some pride." Tomorrow we would visit my sister Amy, which I am sure was one reason for shopping today. You're a lucky man, I thought to myself.

CHAPTER TWENTY-TWO

On the bus to Queens, Kate wanted to know all about Amy. I told her Amy had cared for me after mom died. "In some ways you are much alike," I said. "You both take life as it comes and make the best of it." She held my hand in both of hers as she questioned me. I noticed other men on the bus looking at her lovely face, then quickly looking away. I need not have worried; Kate had eyes only for me.

As we walked up the path to the house, the door opened, and Amy greeted me with a hug. At her side, Thomas shook my hand. We entered, and I drew Kate forward. "Thomas and Amy O'Riley, l would like you to meet Miss Kate Bishop. Kate is Wiley's younger sister, and just recently accepted my proposal of marriage." Amy screamed! Her hands went to her face as tears formed at the corners of her eyes. She threw her arms around Kate, who was also crying.

Thomas was shaking my hand again. "You truly have the luck of the Irish," he said laughing.

The women broke apart, clasping hands. "There's fresh coffee in the kitchen. Come, sit down and tell us the whole story," Amy said.

Thomas left for a moment returning with the newspaper bearing the picture of Wiley and me after the bank robbery. "There's not a cop in Queens that doesn't know about this," he said.

It was the proudest and most memorable day of my life. My sister and my future wife talking and laughing as if they had known each other forever. Meanwhile, Thomas had to know every detail of the robbery. In the wink of an eye, it was three o'clock, and Kate and I had to leave to catch the bus home.

"Amy and I are going to write each other often," Kate said, "and we must visit them again soon. She insisted next time we must bring Wiley along."

"That we shall," I said. "I have the feeling you enjoyed yourself today."

With a bubbling laugh, Kate said, "It was a homecoming. I will have another family to share life with. Amy loves you very much, you know."

"I know," I said, "and I love her. She has never judged me, but often counseled me on being a better person."

"You must have listened well, because that is just what you are," Kate said. I noticed other women looking at us and smiling.

We got home to Hudson Street in time for the corned beef and cabbage special Mattie had promised. It seemed Kate talked non-stop about Amy, telling the family what a grand lady she was.

"Do they plan to have children?" Mattie asked.

"They are hoping children are in the future," Kate said. "She would make a wonderful mother."

After Wiley and I had done the dishes, totally surprising Mattie, we just made the last bus going past the YMCA. "We start our new jobs tomorrow," Wiley reminded me.

"I like the thought of teaching young men to be physically fit," I said, "but it is not a goal I would pursue as my life's work."

"I don't mind being a janitor for now," Wiley said, "but the career I settle on must be much more exciting. Boredom had never suited me."

"We'll start with jumping jacks," I instructed, standing in front of the class. The boys spread out to give themselves some needed space, and we began. Most of the boys were in fair shape. A few could stand to lose some weight; others needed to gain a few pounds. For two hours, we did sit-ups, push-ups, and anything else I could remember from my school days. For the last fifteen minutes, I had them running in a big circle around the gym.

"Times up boys," I said. "Hit the showers and I will see you all tomorrow." As the boys filed out, I saw Tyler standing in the hall doorway.

"You seemed to be enjoying yourself," he said smiling.

"It does me as much good as it does them," I told him.

"Some of the boys do not have an ideal home life," said Tyler. "I am hoping this will bring some discipline and order to their lives."

Nodding my head, I replied, "Whatever, I can do to help you only need to ask."

At supper that night, Wiley and I compared notes. Both jobs had gone well, and Kate and Mattie were both quick to offer advice.

"Does the YMCA hold a Catholic mass?" Mattie asked.

"They do have a small chapel," I told them, "but the services are non-denominational. A Chaplin of sorts allows for any religion to be there. On Saturday a Rabbi comes in."

"How many boys are in your Physical Education class?" Kate asked.

"We started with ten, and now there are fourteen," I said proudly.

"Do they have sports?" asked Wiley.

"A basketball coach is there Saturday and Sunday afternoons," I told him.

The weeks passed quickly, and soon it was Halloween. Sean would take the boys door to door in the neighborhood doing 'treats for the sweet.' This year he was on duty at the firehouse, so Wiley and I volunteered to fill in. Patrick wore a tri-cornered hat, an eye patch and waved a wooden cutlass. Liam had on a black cowboy hat, a silver star pinned to his jacket, and a holstered toy pistol attached to a belt that encircled his waist.

It took about two hours to cover the two-block neighborhood, where the children were everywhere yelling, 'treats for the sweet!' I'm sure Wiley and I had as much fun as they did.

In a few short weeks, it was Thanksgiving day. Kate and I decided to spend the morning with Thomas and Amy. True to her word, Kate informed Wiley that he would come with us.

"I have been wanting to meet your sister," Wiley said. We would return in the afternoon for the turkey dinner With Mattie, Sean, and the boys.

It was great to visit with Amy and Thomas. As Amy, Kate, and I rehashed my childhood, Wiley and Thomas were deep in conversation. They poured over a photo album of Thomas during his cadet training. Wiley had many questions, which Thomas answered eagerly. Soon it was time to leave. On the bus ride home, Wiley was deep in thought.

CHAPTER TWENTY-THREE

With Christmas just a week away, Tyler had purchased a small tree from a corner lot. We set it up in the lobby of the YMCA, and the boys were put to work making decorations. The radio played holiday songs, expanding the festive mood. Piper's Department store donated caps and mittens for gifts on Christmas day. The kitchen would serve a meal to any and all who came to the door.

Amy and Thomas would be getting an electric iron. Pressed uniforms for him, less work for her. Mattie, Sean, and the boys would be enjoying their favorite shows with a new Edison radio. A pocket watch for Wiley seemed the perfect gift. For Kate, an engagement ring. The cost cut into my savings, but for Kate, it was the gift she would treasure.

Christmas morning dawned with a light covering of snow. Wiley and I rode the bus to the Hudson Street home. Walking in, we saw the family gathered around the new radio listening to Christmas carols. I had delivered it the night before to surprise the boys. We sat on the floor by the tree while Kate brought us coffee.

"To my soon-to-be brother-in-law," I said, handing him his gift. When he opened it, his eyes popped wide open, and he laughed. As he did, he handed me my gift. It was almost the identical pocket watch I had given him!

Kate laughed and clapped her hands. "Now you both will always be on time," she exclaimed. I then took the small wrapped box from my coat. Her eyes opened wide as her hands went to her cheeks.

"For my wife-to-be," I said, taking one of her hands and placing the box in the palm. Her hands were shaking as she gently unwrapped the package. The room was silent with every eye on Kate. With great care, Kate opened the box, and the tears welled from her eyes. Ever so gently, she removed the ring and slid it onto the third finger of her left hand.

"It is truly lovely. I adore it, and will wear it with love forever," she said as she gave me a long slow, lingering kiss to last the entire day.

Kate surprised everyone with a gift for Wiley and me. In her hands, she held two envelopes. "I have noticed the boredom gathering in both of your eyes," she said. "The wanderlust has not yet left your souls." Handing us each an envelope, she continued. "The East coast rail lines is offering a special trip on a very special train." Wiley and I opened the envelopes to find two coach tickets.

"This train is known as 'the Orange Blossom Special' and runs from New York to Miami, Florida with only three stops," said Kate.

Wiley and I sat open-mouthed, not sure how to respond. Finally finding my voice, I asked, "Is there work in Florida?"

"Even as we speak, they are harvesting all manner of vegetables and fruit," Kate said.

Examining his ticket, Wiley said, "We leave on January 20th."

"That will give you time to help your employers find replacements," Kate explained, "making it is the proper way to leave."

After morning mass, Kate, Wiley, and I left for Christmas dinner with Thomas and Amy. Wiley had insisted on coming, and we knew he would be welcome. Taking every opportunity to admire her ring, Kate answered every question Wiley and I had about the trip to Miami. Yes, we would need to pack some sandwiches as there was no dining for coach passengers. No, we would not need a winter coat. It would take between thirty-six to forty hours, stops included. Wiley and I would need to do some planning.

Amy had outdone herself. The baked ham and sweet potatoes were excellent, along with the peach pie. Kate proudly showed off her ring, which had the women crying again. Thomas and Wiley seemed to be arguing a point, then laughed and shook hands.

Handing me a wrapped box, Amy said, "Thomas and I thought this would help you both keep the memories alive through the years." Inside was an Eastman Kodak Brownie camera.

"When all the film has been used," explained Amy, "You mail the camera to the company. They develop the film, reload the camera and send it back with the developed pictures." I told Amy about the trip to Miami, saying I would write often.

On the bus home, Wiley was smiling and happy. Kate held my arm as she rested her head on my shoulder. Her eyes were shining as I kissed her goodnight at her door.

If I had prayed to God to find me the perfect woman to spend my life with, he would have found me Kate. I sometimes wondered if our lives were pre-planned by heaven or did we each determine our own destiny. It was one of life's mysteries that was never answered. Late that Christmas night, I fell asleep wondering at the happiness that filled my heart.

CHAPTER TWENTY-FOUR

Wiley, Kate, and I stood outside Grand Central Terminal waiting to board the train. The morning was cool, about thirty degrees. The fall jackets we'd purchased last year kept any cold at bay. I marveled at the huge new engine idling before us— a diesel-run monster, one of the first in America. It pulled storage cars, baggage cars, four Pullman's, a dining car, two coach cars, and others stretching into the distance.

Pulling Wiley's jacket collar up around his neck and giving him a hug, Kate said, "I want you to write me at least three letters before you return." Turning to me, she gave me a tight hug and a long kiss. "I will miss you greatly," she said softly, "but this journey is very important and should be our last separation, God willing. Write many letters. Tell me the sights, sounds and smells of all you see and do." I hugged her tightly as the overhead speakers announced, 'All aboard for Miami, Florida.'

Our coach car had seen better days. It was barely heated, and two windows were cracked. The aisle carpet and many of the seats were threadbare. As we left New York City, the new tall buildings were replaced by tenements and old factories with smokestacks that belched a black grit that clung to every surface it touched.

The train thundered south, through New Jersey on into Pennsylvania where it made one of its scheduled stops in Philadelphia. More passengers boarded the Pullman cars, none for coach. In just under two hours, we were underway again. The beautiful scenery of Maryland gave way to the sprawl of Washington D.C.

I opened my bag and took out the package of food that Kate and Mattie had sent along. We dined on cold-cut sandwiches and a slice of cake apiece, washed down with water from an old water cooler at the end of the car. There were twelve other passengers in our coach: two older married couples traveling together, four men in Marine uniforms, and a farmer with his son. There was also a well-dressed man and woman who seemed out of place. The man carried a satchel, the woman a large handbag. Both appeared quite nervous, and when they talked to each other, it was in low, angry whispers.

Watching them, Wiley murmured, "I don't think those two lovebirds will be with us long."

The train rolled on into Virginia, its next stop in Richmond. It was late evening, and several passengers had fallen asleep. Suddenly, both coach doors. A man in a suit followed by a policeman entered from one end while two more officers entered from the rear. Showing a badge, the man in the suit walked directly up to the well-dressed couple.

"Newton Vance and Emily Green, you are under arrest for the embezzlement of bank money." The policeman handcuffed them and quietly escorted them off the train. The rest of the passengers just sat and stared as they left. Soon the train began moving again, and we all relaxed.

"Better put *that* in your letter to Kate, " Wiley said with a big smile. I made a mental note to do so.

The big drive wheels pulled the train on through the night, across Virginia's rolling countryside. It was warmer now; people took off their coats and used them for pillows. The farmer and his son were deep in conversation with an occasional laugh.

Wiley woke, yawned, stretched, and said, "I could use a few more sandwiches. My stomach is growling." I was thinking how fine a hot cup of coffee would go right now. As I opened my bag for the sandwiches, the coach door opened, and a porter appeared carrying a large gray coffee pot, the fragrant steam wafting from the spout. Behind him, a boy carried a box full of tin cups.

"Thought you folks would like some morning coffee," said the porter with a smile.

The morning sun blazed through the coach windows as the train sped through North Carolina. It slowed down going through Fayetteville, then picked up speed. By late afternoon we crossed into South Carolina. It had warmed up considerably, with a temperature in the high sixties. I got out the last of our sandwiches and passed half to Wiley. We had two apiece.

Wiley nudged my shoulder and said, "The farmer and his son have not eaten since we boarded the train."

I handed Wiley one of my sandwiches. "One of mine and one of yours will do nicely," I said.

Smiling, Wiley took the food and crossed the aisle. Handing them to the farmer, Wiley said, "My friend and I have more than we need and would like to share."

Hesitantly, the farmer accepted. "We thank you kindly," he said, handing a sandwich to his son. The Marines and the two older couples had packed their own food.

It was very early morning when the train made its third scheduled stop in Savannah, Georgia. The farmer, his son, and the Marines left. Now it was only the two older couples with us.

We crossed the Georgia state line and rolled smoothly into Florida. By late morning the diesel engine slowed moving through Jacksonville. At St. Augustine, a ribbon of the ocean was visible to our left. On we went, Daytona Beach, Port Orange, the train taking us ever southward. Then suddenly, it was over. The locomotive slowed when the station came into view— Miami, Florida.

Stepping down from the car, we got slammed by the heat. "It must be at least seventy degrees," said Wiley. Entering the station, we followed the sign to the diner.

A bored-looking waitress walked up. "What can I get ya?" We ordered pancakes and coffee. In minutes we had pancakes smothered in strawberries. There seemed no need for syrup. As we ate, we talked about how to find employment.

"We will need a newspaper and a map," I said. As luck would have it, we didn't need either.

CHAPTER TWENTY-FIVE

"I saw a newspaper stand out on the platform," Wiley said. We walked out and found it empty. Looking around, I noticed several trucks loading crates into a boxcar. On the side of the trucks was a sign, 'Sunshine Produce Company.'

"Hey Wiley, let's find out where those trucks are from," I said. We strolled down, watching the men load the crates. One of the truck drivers sat in the cab with the door open, drinking a bottled cola.

I held out my hand. "Hi, I'm Danny Broome, and this is my friend Wiley Bishop.

Shaking hands, the man said, "Cal Nolan. You boys look really pale. You just come in on the train?"

"Yes we did," Wiley said. "We came from New York looking for work."

"I just might be able to help you." Pointing at the other truck, Cal said, "We haul produce from LaBelle Acres in Lakeland. Right now they're hiring, If you help unload these trucks, I'll give you a ride there."

It took a few hours to get all the crates stacked in the boxcar. From the earthy smell, I was sure it was tomatoes and celery. We finished by early evening. As the crew headed to the diner for supper, Cal spoke up, "Come on along. Evan LaBelle is buying tonight."

As we ate, Cal told us that the LaBelle family farms about a thousand acres of produce. "The family has had the farm for over a hundred years, passed down from generation to generation. They grow and harvest just about every vegetable you can name. Right now it's tomatoes and celery. In a few weeks it will be carrots and green beans."

I rode with Cal, and Wiley rode with a driver named Jim Duprey. Cal wanted to know what it was like living in New York.

"Right now it's bad," I said, "Thousands of people and no work. The soup kitchens try to feed as many as they can, but still many go hungry."

"Do the people with money help at all," asked Cal.

"Many do, but the need is so great that many still go without," I told him. As I looked out, the beams of the headlights made the road look white. Seeing my frown, Cal laughed. "In the south, we pave the roads with crushed clam and oyster shells," he said. "It solves two problems. It gets rid of thousands of shells and we don't have to buy gravel." It was midnight when we turned off the road onto the LaBelle Acres drive. "You and Wiley grab an empty bunk and I'll let Evan know you're here."

CLANG! CLANG! CLANG! Someone was banging on a metal triangle. Checking my pocket watch, it was 7 a.m. "Breakfast time! Get it while it's hot!" At the mention of food, Wiley jumped up and was out the door with me right behind. We followed the others to the food tent. Plank tables with benches filled the white canvas tent. Pots of coffee, platters of pancakes and bacon, and bowls of fresh fruit were waiting.

The man next to me held out his hand. "I'm Arnie Madison," he said. "You boys must have come in last night with the produce trucks."

"We rode in with Cal Nolan," I said. "He told us they needed workers."

"He was right about that," said Arnie. "We need tomato pickers right now."

A portly man with white hair and glasses approached, followed by a younger woman carrying a ledger. "I'm looking for the two men who came in on the trucks last night with Cal Nolan," he said.

Wiley and I stepped forward. "That would be us, sir," I told him. "My name is Danny Broome and this is my friend Wiley Bishop. Cal said you would be hiring workers."

The younger woman wrote our names in her ledger. "What kind of work have you done?" As I told of our work experience, they both nodded their heads, looked at each other, and then turned back to us. "You can start today. We must get the tomatoes to market. Your pay is $1.50 a day. My foreman Ted Weems will get you started."

The fields of produce looked as if they went on forever. Ted took us out to a tomato field where many other people were already picking. Handing us baskets, he showed us where to start and then left. It was like old times. We moved down the rows filling the baskets with the bright red tomatoes and taking them to the end of the row for pick up.

Ahead of me and a few rows over, a woman sang an old church hymn called 'Down by the Riverside.' Several other voices would join in on the chorus. When the song was over, there was a silence broken only by the people and baskets moving ahead. Then a deep male voice began singing 'Bringing in the Sheaves.' This time a female chorus joined in. The songs bought a timeless rhythm to the tedious labor. I found myself humming as the basket filled with ripe tomatoes. Then I heard Wiley softly singing along. Tonight this would all go into the letter to Kate.

CHAPTER TWENTY-SIX

By the end of February, we were harvesting new red potatoes and radishes. Wiley and I were no longer the pale-skinned boys from New York. We were tanned and seasoned produce workers. Coming in from the field one Saturday, we found Ted Weems waiting for us. Handing us our pay envelopes, he asked, "How would you like to take a break from the produce picking?"

"What do you have in mind?" I asked.

"Come, sit in the shade and I will explain." Following Ted to a picnic table under two palm trees, we sat and listened. "Evan's nephew, Andre LaBelle, runs a commercial fishing business on the coast at Clearwater. Four of his boat crew quit over a wage dispute." Leaning forward, he continued. "Andre managed to hire one local but needs at least two more. He called Evan this morning for help. Would you be interested?"

"It would be a new work experience for us," I told him, "but if the pay is right I would try it." I looked at Wiley, who nodded his head.

"It pays two dollars per day per man," said Ted, "I have a truck waiting to take you to Clearwater, so pack your bags." Fifteen minutes later, we were on the road.

Andre LaBelle was waiting at the harbor when we arrived. Shaking our hands, he said, "So, you men want to be fishermen?"

"We have no experience, but we are hard workers," I said.

"This I know," Andre said, "I asked Uncle Evan for two hard workers and he sent you. Come with me." We walked down to the seawall where two big boats bobbed on the tide. "These are my life," he said. "The near boat is 'Viola', and the far one is 'Betina'. They are both forty-foot long with inboard Chrysler engines. With these I supply the restaurants with the freshest fish in Florida."

"Is there a place we can sleep?" I asked.

Pointing toward the town, Andre said, "The only place is the Mariner's Hotel. The clerk will give you both a weekly rate of five dollars, total. They have a small café where you can eat."

"When do we start?" Wiley asked.

"Be here at sunrise, Monday morning," Andre said, "and we will make you into fishermen!"

The inboard engines of the boats were at a rumbling idle as we pulled away from the dock. When we got clear of the harbor, they came to life with a steady roar. The boat lifted and dropped as we rode over the waves. I was on board the 'Viola,' while Wiley went on the 'Betina.'

A dark young man approached, holding out his hand. "I'm Joe," he said. "You'll be working with me." He handed me a pair of leather gloves with rubberized palms. "You will need these later. Soon we'll let out the nets, then give them time to sink down." Pointing to a large two-handled windlass, he explained. "When the time is right, we reel in the nets. The fish that are caught we throw into the hold."

"What kind of fish?" I asked.

"Lately, it's mostly grouper and sea bass. You'll catch on quick."

"Why did the other men quit?" I asked.

Turning very serious, Joe answered. "As you may have noticed I am Indian, Seminole Indian to be exact. Andre pays us all the same wage. Those who quit thought I should be paid less or that whites should be paid more. Andre told them he paid according to their work, not their race."

"Andre is right," I said, "and I hope we can be friends."

A smile spread across his face. "I think I like you, Danny Broome," he said and then laughed.

Including myself, there were seven crewmen. We took turns working the windlass and pulling the large fish from the net. Along with the fish came all manner of junk from the ocean floor—metal cans, glass bottles, a headlight from a car, a bald rubber tire, a leather boot, clumps of seaweed, and even a large turtle.

Joe threw it in the hold, saying, "they make a great soup!" When the nets were empty, they were slowly let out again to bring in more fish. The junk was picked up from the scuppers and tossed into a large barrel secured to the deck. Jugs of fresh water were passed around as the crew watched the hold fill with fish. The sun was hot, but the breeze from the west was steady and welcome.

The nets were in, and the hold was almost full as the big boat turned and headed for port. The crew was relaxed and curious about me and where I was from. I noticed about half the crew were Seminoles. Andre came on deck and asked, "So, man from New York, how do you like being a fisherman?"

"I will be ready to go again tomorrow," I said.

Speaking up, Joe said, "He worked hard and learned quick. I say we keep him." Everyone laughed and slapped my back.

"My Uncle Evan loves me," Andre said, "and sends me only the best."

I was waiting on the dock as the 'Betina' moored next to us. Wiley looked a little tired but was smiling as he joined me.

"How did it go?" I asked.

"Well, the captain, Antoine, said I could come back tomorrow," Wiley said with a laugh. We unloaded the holds. The fish went into baskets and onto the trucks bound for the markets and restaurants of west Florida.

After a hot shower at the hotel and a meal at the café, we returned to the room. "Kate is expecting a letter from you," I reminded him.

"And she shall have it tonight while the memory of today is fresh in my mind," Wiley said.

I wrote two letters. Amy and Kate would each hear of the produce workers turned fishermen. I knew this would not be my life's work, but the experience was well worth the labor.

March sped toward April as Wiley and I helped fish the Gulf of Mexico. Our tan deepened, our muscles adjusted to the new workload. It was something I knew I would never forget, a story for the children Kate wanted, as did I. Wiley seemed to have gained a new confidence. It showed in his walk and softer smile. Sherrie, the young waitress at the café, was completely smitten with Wiley. Her mother was the cook and kept a close eye on her daughter, but Wiley never stepped out of line or encouraged her. Sherrie finally settled on Wiley as a friend.

CHAPTER TWENTY-SEVEN

The last day of March fell on a Friday. "Today we do not go out for fish," Andre said with a worried frown. "They are forecasting a tropical storm." Joe was at the end of the dock, watching the horizon and the ocean waves.

Turning, he told Andre, "This will be more than just a storm."

It was a hurricane. The wind steadily increased with bouts of slashing rain. "Tie everything down, then head for the hotel," Andre shouted over the rising wind. The palm trees bent almost double as the wind tore through them. Huge waves slammed the shore as we all ran for the hotel.

"There is a root cellar out back," yelled one of the men. We ran for the back door just as the front window blew out. Joe yanked on the cellar door, trying to get it open.

"Someone is holding it from inside," he hollered. I grabbed the handle with him, and we yanked as hard as we could, pulling Sherrie's mother off her feet.

"Let go of the door and let us in," hollered Andre. All seven of us managed to fit into the cellar with Sherrie, her mother, and the desk clerk, with only a kerosene lantern for light. We secured the cellar door with a rope and listened to the damaging storm outside: the screech of metal roofs being torn off, the splintery crash of wood as the wind destroyed buildings. It seemed to go on for hours. Then there was a lull in the deafening noise.

"It's the eye of the storm," Andre said, "now the full fury is coming."

BOOM! Crash! Bang! Rain raced in around the door as the wind tried to tear it off its hinges. *CRASH!* Something heavy fell across the door, sealing us inside. No one spoke; there were no words for what was happening. Then the wind began to die down, like a dying man fighting for his last breath. The rain lessened, the noise slowly eased up, and then it was over.

An uprooted palm tree had fallen across the cellar door. With three of us pushing, we managed to roll the tree off and open the door. We emerged from the cellar, ten of us who had lived through a hurricane. The scene was one of total destruction. The hotel was gone, torn from its concrete floor and spread all over the landscape. One palm tree was still standing, leaning at an awkward angle with roots showing. The town of Clearwater was almost completely gone.

Andre stumbled to the beach where the 'Viola' lay on its side, the cabin torn off. There was no sign of the 'Betina.' The dock was gone, only a few pilings poking up through the water. On what had been the Main street lay a truck on its cab. Next to it was a bathtub broken in half. We would learn later that the hurricane had swept northeast across the state, cutting a twenty-mile wide path of death and destruction until moving out into the Atlantic. Wiley and I looked at each other, both knowing our days of fishing in the gulf were over.

Disaster help began arriving from all over the state. The first to arrive was Evan LaBelle, with tents, food, and barrels of fresh water. Evan cried as he hugged Andre, who was also leaking tears of joy. We all pitched in and cleared an area for the tents. A fire pit was dug and laid with charcoal. Cooking pots were soon bubbling over the glowing coals as the wonderful smell of cooking food spread over the makeshift campsite.

Searchers were out looking for survivors. Other cellars opened, and people began to take a count of survivors. By nightfall, only three had not been accounted for. Evan had called the Governor's office, who promised relief would arrive by tomorrow. Until then, we prayed as a group for those missing, and then we ate.

One of the crew, Dennis Hobart, sat with Wiley and me as we ate. He was a lanky tow-haired man a few years older than us who had crewed on the 'Betina.'

"I wish now I had stayed in Georgia," he said, "but I always wanted to be a fisherman."

"Where in Georgia are you from?" I asked.

"Just a small town called Meigs, right off Highway 19. I used to work for a big farm there, growing and harvesting turnips Vidalia onions."

"Are you thinking of going back to Meigs?" I asked.

"Oh no," he said, "I'll move on up the coast and hire on to another boat. This is where I belong." Later, Wiley and I talked it over and decided on going to Georgia.

"We had planned to eventually anyway," Wiley said. "Now seems like the perfect time."

The following morning we told Andre and Evan we were moving on. "It's sad this happened, but if you ever come back to Florida, you come to me first. I will always have work for you." Andre handed us each a ten-dollar bill, shook our hands, and wished us luck. We walked out to the highway and caught a ride north.

CHAPTER TWENTY-EIGHT

A farmer and his wife gave us a ride to Perry. "We were looking at a small place near the Gulf," the farmer said, "but after that hurricane, I think we'll keep the farm a while."

Wiley and I ate at a diner in Perry, then walked back out to the highway. A trucker slowed, then stopped.

"Where you men heading?" he asked.

"We heard there is work in Meigs," Wiley told him.

"Well, climb on in. I'm going as far as Thomasville. Meigs is just up the road from there." He asked if we had been in the path of the hurricane. I told him about Clearwater and how we had lost everything we owned.

"I can help you there," he said. "The First Baptist church in Thomasville takes clothing donations. I'll drop you off and you can get almost everything you need."

The ladies at the First Baptist Church took us to a storage shed behind the church. Inside, we found pants and shirts to fit. Our boots were in passable shape, but we would need hats. We found a short brim Stetson for Wiley and a black Fedora for me. Everything went into an old leather carryall. We tried to pay, but the money was politely declined.

Walking through town, we located a dime-store where we purchased razors, socks, underwear, combs, toothbrushes, and paste, along with pencils, paper, and one small packet of envelopes. Kate would get a letter she would not expect.

We stayed the night at the Thomasville Hotel, one dollar per night, each. The man at the desk said, "The diner is still open if you men are hungry," We feasted on chicken and dumplings and a slice of apple pie with coffee.

Later, in our room, after a bath and shave, we felt human again. I wrote to Kate, telling her about the hurricane and our move to Georgia. Tomorrow we would again be produce harvesters. I was asleep as soon as I lay down.

If you ever want information in a small town, there are three to ask: the bartender, the waitress, and the hotel desk clerk.

"Grover Jantz is the man you want to see," the desk clerk said. "He's got the biggest turnip farm in the county. Take Highway 19 north for five miles. You can't miss the sign."

Wiley and I stuck out our thumbs and immediately got a ride from a local farmer. He dropped us off at the sign that said 'Jantz Farms.' Walking up the drive, we heard the tractor in the field pulling the digger. A truck was unloading baskets of big onions at a warehouse. The sliding double doors were open, so we walked inside.

Four men were bagging onions in fifty-pound bags. A chubby man chewing on a cigar looked us over. "You boys looking for work?" he asked.

"Yes, we are, and we have done this kind of work before," I added.

Grinning around the cigar, he replied, "I'm Grover Jantz, I pay a dollar a day and meals." He pulled a notebook from his back pocket and wrote down our names. "Let's see what you can do."

Setting our travel bag down by the door, I picked a sack from the pile and held it as Wiley filled it. I tied off the top and took another. With a chuckle, Grover said, "You're hired," and then walked away.

Vidalia onions have a unique odor. It's earthy and pungent that leaves a trace of itself on whatever it touches, especially clothing. We bagged onions for a week and a half, and when done, Grover said he'd start us on turnips the next day.

One of the older workers, Lee Mayer, wanted to know about the hurricane. The other three workers gathered around as Wiley gave a very graphic account of our survival.

Produce trucks arrived and departed every afternoon. On a hunch, I asked one of the drivers if there were more big farms farther north. He thought for a moment, lifted his hat, and scratched his bald spot. "In Georgia, it's just onions and turnips, but just across the state line in Alabama, outside a town called Anniston, the lettuce harvest will start in about two weeks."

Later, I mentioned it to Wiley. "I'm ready to go whenever you are," he said. "Anything that doesn't smell like onions will be fine with me."

We bagged turnips day after day for two weeks. Finally, the last bags went out on the truck, and the job was done. Grover paid us Thursday afternoon and said, "I expect you men will be moving on."

I told him about Anniston, Alabama, and he nodded his head. "Trent Farms is the place you mean. Harlan Trent grows three hundred acres of lettuce every year. Tell him I sent you."

We packed up, said goodbye to Lee and the other men, and walked out to the highway.

CHAPTER TWENTY-NINE

A couple on their way to visit relatives in Macon gave us a ride to the bus station. Two one-way tickets to Anniston cost $1.50 each. The bus left the following morning at seven.

"Is there a second-hand clothing store nearby?" I asked the clerk.

"I believe there's one up on Beech Avenue, just a block over."

We found the store and proceeded to stock up on clothes. At $4.00, we found a canvas bag with a drawstring, good boots, and a belt. Wiley even found packages of men's underwear and socks, new and in the wrapper.

"Factory seconds," the clerk told us. "Beats throwing them away."

Across the street was a run-down hotel. A room with two beds and a bath at the end of the hall cost a dollar.

"Everything that smells of onions I'm throwing away," Wiley said. "They are worn out, anyway." I agreed. After a dollar meal at a diner, it was back to the hotel.

"Write Kate and Mattie a letter tonight," I reminded Wiley.

"And we need to get a money order," Wiley said.

"We can get one tomorrow morning in Anniston."

"I wonder will be ready after the lettuce?"

Smiling, I answered, "Peaches, my friend. Imagine your clothes smelling like peaches."

"What a glorious thought," Wiley sighed.

A tall man in a blue shirt wearing a white Panama hat was my first impression of Harlan Trent. "If Grover sent you, then you must be good workers," he said. "Ever harvest lettuce?"

"No sir," I answered. "Cucumbers, tomatoes, potatoes, onions and a few other vegetables. Also apples and pears."

Pointing to a row of Army surplus tents, he said, "Pay is a dollar a day. Find an empty bunk and I'll have my foreman Lyle get you started."

Lyle Parker wrote our names in his book and took us out to the field. "The lettuce heads are already cut loose from the root. Strip off the outer broad leaves, fill the wheel barrows and take them to the end of the row." The lettuce looked like green bowling balls but not as heavy. Ahead of us, three men with machetes lifted the heads, cutting them loose. Wiley and I followed, each with a wheelbarrow, and went to work.

We ran into some old friends that evening. Jake and Estelle Burnett and their daughter Loretta, about halfway through her pregnancy, with no young man in sight. Wiley and I smiled, said hello, but received only an angry stare from Estelle.

"Somewhere, a young man is running for his life," Wiley said.

"I would pass half the blame on to Estelle," I told him. Nodding his head, Wiley agreed. Frank from Ohio was also there. True to his word, he had worked in only the southern states. We told him about the peach harvest coming up. "I know just the place. It's outside of Lafayette. Orley's Orchard has acres and acres of peach trees, probably six different varieties."

"Why grow six kinds of peaches?" Wiley asked.

Frank smiled and said, "Because they ripen at different times. When one kind has all been picked, another kind is ready." It sounded like this job could last a while.

The last of the lettuce was hauled away on Saturday afternoon. It was the end of April, and the heat was intense. After getting paid, Wiley and I got a ride into Anniston. Slipping a dollar to the desk clerk got us a bath and shave. Then we thumbed a ride to Lafayette. An almost new Ford V-8 stopped. A boy was driving it—sandy-haired, thin, with a tooth missing in front. "How far are you goin'?" he asked.

"Just to Lafayette," Wiley said. Something didn't seem quite right, but we weren't going far, so we climbed into the back. The boy took off like he was in a race.

"Nice car," I said, "Is it yours?"

Laughing, the boy yelled over his shoulder, "Not hardly. The man I was working for didn't pay me, so I borrowed his car!"

The speed got up to seventy-five, then I heard the siren between Wiley's prayers: "We are going to jail! Jesus help us, we are going to jail!" Going too fast to make a sharp curve, the Ford crashed through a barbed-wire fence and out into a grassy field where a big oak tree stood in the center. The boy tried to turn the car, but it slid along on the grass. Knowing what was coming, I grabbed Wiley by the shirt and dragged him down on the floor with me.

CRASH!

The car skid, slamming into the tree on the front passenger side. Dazed, I sat up and checked on Wiley. Other than a bump on his head and my skinned knee, we were fine. Both back doors had sprung open on impact, and we climbed out. The police parked their cars on the road and raced toward us across the field, with their guns drawn.

Out of breath and gasping, one of them wheezed out, "Hands up! Hands up!" The other officer opened the driver's door, and the boy fell out, laughing. A gash on his forehead oozed blood, and his left leg was bent at an awkward angle.

CHAPTER THIRTY

Wiley and I carried the boy to the police car, and one of them drove him to the hospital in Anniston, then to jail. They knew Billy had been alone when he stole the vehicle, so believing our story wasn't a problem.

"That little jerk has been nothing but trouble since he learned to walk," the cop told us. Then he asked where we were headed.

"Orley's Orchards is hiring peach pickers, so that's where we need to go."

"Hey," he sniffed, "that's only a few miles from here. I'll give you a ride."

Wiley's praying had paid off. We were not going to jail.

Peach blossoms have a very distinctive smell, and they tickled my not as we walked up the drive. Wiley inhaled deeply, his eyes closed. "I think this will be a very pleasant harvest," he said. More Army surplus tents with folding cots would be home for a while.

A well-built blonde woman of middle age, about five foot ten, carrying a clipboard approached us. "My name is Libby, You here for pickin'?" she asked.

"Yes we are," I said. "When do you start?"

She wrote down. "Pay is a dollar a day. We start Monday morning right after breakfast."

As we sat on our cots, a few of the men joined us. Their stories were much like ours. Aaron from Chicago, about our age, Clayton from Detroit, middle-aged, Bill from Milwaukee, Leonard from Rapid City, all on the move across the nation trying to earn enough money just to stay alive. All were single, all were making the best of a bad economy.

Picking peaches was like picking apples or pears, except you had to be gentler because they bruised easily. The process was simple: from the tree to the bag, from bag to the basket, then onto the trucks. Libby kept count of the number of baskets going out and to which wholesaler. I noticed none of the truckers argued with her. Libby looked like she could hold her own.

A light rain fell overnight, hardly enough to dampen the soil. The drought was persisting. There was more talk about the dust storms out west. The wind coming down from Canada sought the dry earth and lifting it into the thermal atmosphere like a brown cloud. I felt that we would be better off staying in the south and Midwest to find work. Many of the large farms irrigated from deep wells. These would be the places to seek out.

Wiley and I spent two months picking peaches. On Saturday, July third, the last truck was loaded and rolled away. Libby handed out pay, and when she got to us, she said, "You two hang around a few minutes, I want to talk to you."

About ten minutes later, she motioned us over to the shade of an Oak tree where four chairs awaited. Clayton from Detroit was already seated. "The owner, Mr. Orley is going to build some bunkhouses," Libby began. "These old Army tents are almost used up. A crew is coming Monday to lay out forms for the cement floors." Looking around at the four of us, she continued. "I know Sunday is July fourth and most people will be celebrating, but I need these tents gone, tomorrow." We all looked at each other, knowing what was coming.

Libby pointed a finger at each of us and said, "Working on a Sunday pays another dollar, and because it's a holiday, Mr. Orley will pay another two dollars. That's four dollars each for a day's work." Libby was smiling now, knowing she had us.

"What do we do with the tents?" I asked.

She tapped the clipboard lightly on her knee. "When the tents are collapsed, save the poles, they might come in handy for something else. The tents get loosely folded. Then we pour kerosene on them and burn them. We tried giving them away, but no one wants them, so we burn them. The cots get folded up and stored. We will need them later. On Monday morning the three of you can hire on as carpenter's helpers—just fetch and carry what the builders need. Still a dollar a day, but at least a month's work for all three of you."

Libby, Wiley, Clayton, and I ate the last meal served in the cook tent. Coffee, biscuits and gravy, and sliced peaches swimming in heavy cream. Then we got started. The tent pegs were pulled, the poles removed, the sides folded in, and the tent folded into an untidy pile. They would be burned where they lay. One by one, kerosene was poured over the canvas and then lit on fire. On a July day in Alabama, the temperature will average about ninety-five degrees. Add the burning tents, and the heat was almost unbearable. By sundown, piles of smoldering ashes remained, the last few embers just red dots winking up through the graying smoke.

We slept on the covered porch of the Orley house that night. I wrote Kate a letter telling her all that was happening. I was missing her badly, needing the touch of her hand, the sweet smell of her hair as we hugged, the quiet love that shone from her eyes. The emotion was as old as time but new to me. Memories of Kate gathered in my mind. The proposal, the ring at Christmas, her first meeting with Amy—all the times when my heart felt too big for my chest because of Kate. I closed my eyes and slept.

I awoke to the sound of hammering. The sun was barely up, Wiley was still asleep. I nudged him with my foot.

"Time to start the day," I yawned. Clayton was already up and dressed. Libby brought out hot coffee from the kitchen.

"I have a lot of trucks coming today," she said. "The cement trucks will be here soon, then truckloads of lumber to unload. Then more trucks with the doors and windows."

"Where do we put all that stuff?" Clayton asked.

With a big grin, Libby replied, "Finish that coffee and I'll show you." Libby must have been up working before sunrise. She had placed sticks in the ground with paper attached, marking the spots for each delivery. At that moment, I realized that Mr. Orley did not pay Libby her worth as his foreman.

CHAPTER THIRTY-ONE

Building something was a new experience for both Wiley and me. Although we would not be using the tools to build, we still would be part of the construction. The cement pads had been poured and set. Now the carpenters were framing the buildings. Working as teams, Wiley and I, and Libby and Clayton, toted two by fours, moved ladders, and kept the builders supplied with nails. After the framing, the roof trusses went up and were nailed in place. Next were the outer walls. We moved stacks of boards to keep the carpenters supplied. The windows and doors went in, and the roofs were laid. Over this went the tin roofing. Hour after hour, day after day, each building took shape.

As we worked, I noticed a bond forming between Libby and Clayton. Wiley noticed too.

"I don't think Clayton will be leaving anytime soon," he commented.

"For everyone there is someone," I said. "Even you, although you have not met the right one yet."

July was almost over when the bunkhouses were completed. It was Thursday afternoon when the carpenters packed up and left. Libby handed us our pay envelopes, saying, "Mr. Orley was so pleased with your work that you will find a few extra dollars have been added. I want to thank both of you for seeing this project to its completion."

Libby then handed me another envelope. "My friends Gilley and Louise Stover own a large watermelon and cantaloupe farm in Warren, Arkansas. They are harvesting now. Inside are directions and two bus tickets. Clayton will drive you to Lafayette." We shook hands, packed what few things we had, got in the truck with Clayton, and were off.

Clayton dropped us off at the bank in Lafayette. I got a fifty-dollar money order to send to Kate, and Wiley and I each had ten dollars left.

"Let's stay the night, get cleaned up and sleep in a real bed," I said.

"A good meal wouldn't hurt either," Wiley replied.

The Lafayette Hotel was the only one in town. When we checked in, I saw a sign posted on the wall behind the desk that read: WASH AND DRY, 50 CENTS. Pointing at the sign, I asked the lady at the desk, "Could we bring down a load of clothes to be washed?"

"You certainly may. My daughter does the washing. Your clothes will be waiting outside your door in the morning."

The beds were soft but comfortable. The bathroom had a shower, which felt wonderful. On the way out, we dropped off our clothes on the way to Luke's Café, which was two doors down and not too busy. A big slice of ham, fried potatoes, cream corn, apple, and iced tea with ice in it! We then decided to watch a western movie called 'Border Law' starring Buck Jones at the Bijou theatre.

Back at the hotel, I propped myself up in bed and began a letter to Kate, telling her we would be going to Arkansas. I wrote about helping to build the bunkhouses and burning the old tents. Wiley was reading a newspaper he had picked up in the lobby.

"Any good news?' I asked.

"The President says the worst is over and things should be getting better soon," he replied. I just smiled. It was the same thing he said two months ago.

As promised, our clean clothes were in a basket outside our door the next morning. We packed up and checked out at the desk. A younger woman was there, so I asked, "Are you the daughter who washed our clothes?"

Blushing a little, she said, "Yes I am. Is everything alright?"

"Everything is fine. In fact, you did a wonderful job, worth a dollar at least." I handed her the dollar, and her smile lit up the room. She gave us directions to the bus station and waved as we left.

Another hot day with no rain in sight. I had the bus window half-open to catch a breeze as we crossed the state line into Arkansas. In a few hours, we slowed, then stopped in the town of Warren. I reread the directions from Libby. The farm was six miles out on a county road. We had barely started walking when a car, driven by an older man, stopped. He asked, "You men going to Stover's farm?"

"That we are," Wiley replied.

"I'm Gilley Stover. If you are looking for work I sure could use the help." We got in the car, and I handed him the note from Libby. As he read it, he chuckled a bit then said, "If Libby says your good workers, then it's my good luck."

The cantaloupes were ripe and ready. Wiley and I loaded them into wheelbarrows and took them to the end of the row, where a truck waited. We handed the cantaloupes up to two men in the back of the truck who packed them into crates. Stacked four crates high, the truck would deliver the melons to the boxcar at the rail yard for shipment north. The day was hot and humid, and off to the west, a brown haze was spreading. A dust storm was growing.

It took two weeks to harvest the cantaloupes; then, the watermelons were ready. No crates for these big melons. They were stacked in the truck as high as the sides allowed. They were heavy, awkward, and often slippery with sweat. Day by day, we worked to clear the fields. A cart, pulled by a donkey and driven by a boy, brought a milk can of water with a dipper hanging on the side. Now and then, from across the field, you could hear someone holler, "Need some water over here!" As one truck was filled and left, another would take its place. Finally, on a Friday about noon, the last melon was lifted into the truck, and the job was done.

Wiley and I were last in line to get paid. As Gilley handed us the money, he said, "I know a man in Lebanon, Missouri, his name is Tony Ketchum. He grows four hundred acres of beets every year. He should be starting his harvest any day." We thanked him and caught a ride into Warren.

"I think we should keep moving east," Wiley said. "That dust cloud is growing." I nodded my head in agreement. In Warren, we got bus tickets to Lebanon for a dollar each.

"Bus leaves at six this evening," the clerk said. A block up the street, we saw a café. Sandwiches and coffee would hold us till Lebanon.

CHAPTER THIRTY-TWO

Tony was six feet tall and all muscle. His tanned skin rippled with every move he made. Then you noticed his smile and friendly eyes. "You men want to work in the field or be baggers?" he asked.

"We probably would be best at bagging," I said, "because we have done it before. Potatoes, turnips and beets."

"Fine with me," Tony said. "We start tomorrow morning." Wiley and I had arrived Sunday afternoon. We got a ride from town with a circuit preacher on his way to another small church. Another folding cot in another surplus Army tent would be our home for at least two weeks.

As strong as the urge was to get back on the road in January, it was stronger now to begin working our way home to New Jersey. I wrote a letter to Kate after supper letting her know where we were and would be working our way east. Wiley was lying on his cot, staring at the canvas roof.

"We should be thinking of working our way home," he sighed.

"What would you do if you were home?" I asked.

"This time, I would stay there," he answered.

Four hundred acres of beets took three weeks to harvest. Well, that's what it took our crew. The problem was Amos Blake. Amos was a big man, about six foot two, who showed up with two friends, all very friendly at first. All three chose to work in the field, following the digger and loading the baskets for pick up. Amos only had one speed—slow—and his friends, Toby and Jack, could barely keep up with him.

Tony cautioned them politely the first week. "You need to pick up your pace men." By Wednesday of the second week, Tony's warning got tougher. "If you can't go any faster, I will have to let you go." Saturday at noon, Amos, Toby, and Jack got fired.

Amos did not take it well. "I work as hard as everybody," he yelled.

Handing him his pay, Tony said softly, "All three of you pack up and leave." Amos slapped the pay from Tony's hand and took a swing at him! It couldn't really be called a fight. With one punch, Tony laid Amos out in the dirt. Toby and Jack stood there with mouths open, not believing what they saw.

"Pick him up and go," Tony said. In fifteen minutes, all three were on the road.

Tony took their place in the field and did the work of three men. Us baggers had to really go to keep up. On Friday of the third week, the crop was in.

On payday, Tony told us, "There is a guy I know in Benton, Kentucky who is ready to bring in his crop of sweet potatoes. Tell him Tony sent you."

A produce truck gave us a lift to the bus station in town. I took a half dollar from my pants pocket and showed it to

Wiley. "Heads, we stay here overnight, tails we go right on to Benton."

"I'll catch it in the air," Wiley said. With my thumb, I sent the coin spinning straight up. As it reached its peak and started down, Wiley picked it from the air, slapping it down on the back of his other hand. Slowly lifting his hand, he smiled and showed it to me. It was tails.

We entered the station and looked at the map on the wall. At the counter, Wiley told the clerk, "Two one way tickets to Benton, Kentucky."

Checking his book, the clerk said, "Tickets are a dollar fifty each, bus leaves at seven." Just enough time to get a meal.

Halfway to Benton, the bus decided it needed a rest. It choked, sputtered, choked again, and quit. The driver sat there and hung his head for a minute, then, opening the door, he got up.

"I need someone to hold the flashlight while I look at the motor," he said.

"I'll go," said Wiley. He and the driver got out, opened the hood, and stared at the motor. After some tinkering, the driver came in, turned the key, and it started, then it quit again. A man sitting in the back woke up and asked, "Why aren't we moving?"

"Something wrong with the motor," I said. Muttering under his breath, the man got up and walked out of the bus. After about ten minutes, the driver came back in, turned the key, and the bus started and kept running. The hood slammed shut, and Wiley and the man came in and sat down. The man went back to sleep, and the bus was moving again.

"What was the problem?" I asked Wiley.

"The fuel filter was dirty," Wiley said. "That other guy took it out, cleaned it and put it back in. He told the driver to get a new one in Benton." The bus got into the station after midnight.

The town was quiet, the bus station was open but empty. "The clerk comes in at five every morning," the driver said. "Might as well stretch out on an empty bench and get some sleep."

The clerk woke us up at five. "The diner's just opened a block over on Maple street," he said. "They got biscuits and gravy this morning." Stiff and sore from the hardwood bench, Wiley and I picked up our bags and walked out.

CHAPTER THIRTY-THREE

Hot coffee, biscuits, and gravy, served by a pretty girl with a smile, whose name was Nancy— a fine way to start the day.

"Where is the big sweet potato farm?" I asked her.

"That would be Vernon Talbot," she said. "His farm is six miles out on the county road."

Talbot's farm was already busy when we arrived because of the goat. A paunchy older man swinging a notebook was yelling, "Somebody get a rope on him!" If anyone got close, the goat would lower his head with the big curved horns and charge! Looking around, I saw the Talbot's vegetable garden next to the house. I stepped over, pulled two carrots, and then stepped back.

"Everyone, quiet down," I said, "and get me a long piece of rope." Getting as close as I dared, I knelt on one knee and tossed a carrot to the goat. It landed right in front of his nose. He sniffed it, then picked it up and ate it. I waved the other carrot at him. "If you liked that," I said softly, "here's another." Wiley nudged me in the back with his knee and dropped a length of rope by my hand.

The goat strolled up to me and stopped. I broke the carrot in half and fed half to the goat. As he ate, I slipped the rope around his neck. I stood up and started slowly walking toward the barn, with the goat following, keeping his eye on the other half of the carrot. The man with the notebook motioned me forward toward a pen with the gate open. As we walked through the gate, I gave the goat the other half of the carrot, untied the rope, and left the pen. Someone closed and latched the gate.

Turning around, I asked, "Which of you is Vernon Talbot?" The man with the notebook had a big smile on his pudgy face as he stuck out his hand.

"If you are looking for work, you're hired," he said.

Vernon had fashioned bag stands. Using two by fours, the frame held the fifty-pound bag secure while two men filled it. Then the bag was tied off and set outside to wait for the trucks. Four men could do the work of six, and faster. When the produce trucks came in the afternoon, we all helped load.

One of the other workers, Hank, from Kansas, told us, "When this is done, there is a big pumpkin farm in Compton, Kentucky that will be hiring. We can get a ride with Wilbur and Betty Harris if we help with the gas money." I talked to Wilbur later and arranged a ride for us.

Wilbur Harris had built a small house on the back of his flatbed truck. The bed folded up when it was not in use, and the table folded down. A storage box with a lid held the food, another held clothing, and a third was for the pots and pans. It was ideal for traveling and living in if you didn't go too far north. Hank, Wiley, and I rode in the house to Compton. It cost us a dollar in gas, well worth the trip.

The pumpkin harvest lasted two weeks. It was now the end of September, and the nights were getting cooler. I wrote Kate a letter telling her we were going to West Virginia and would soon be home. Spencer, West Virginia was another sweet potato harvest Hank had told us about. He was going back south to Georgia with the Harris's.

Wiley and I boarded the bus in Compton at two in the afternoon. It was getting close to sundown when we crossed into West Virginia. Suddenly two police cars with lights and sirens flew past us. The bus slowed but kept going. As we topped a small hill, we saw a roadblock ahead. A cop waved the bus driver to stop. Pulling to the left as far as he could, the driver let the bus idle and got out to talk to the cop. Another police car drove up. An officer and a man in a suit got out to talk to the bus driver and the other cop. Then the driver came back to let us know what was going on.

Standing in the aisle, the driver told us, "We may be here a while folks. Two men robbed the bank in Weston, about thirty miles north east. The police have them boxed in right here." Taking off his hat and wiping his brow with his sleeve, he added, "The police want me to back up a half mile just to be safe. There will probably be some shooting." As the driver sat down and started backing up, the shooting began!

Two pistol shots rang out first, followed by a shotgun blast. Then the steady rat-tat-tat of a machine gun. More pistol shots and another shotgun blast. All this as the bus driver was backing up the hill. Then all was quiet. There were six people on the bus, plus the driver. We all sat and stared at each other, waiting for something to happen.

One of the cops walked to the center of the road and waved the bus driver forward. Slowly, the bus rolled down the hill until it stopped even with the cop. The bus door opened, and the cop stepped in.

"It's all over folks," he said. "The two bank robbers are dead."

CHAPTER THIRTY-FOUR

The police cleared a path in the road for the bus to get through. Moving slowly past the carnage, we saw one body lying in front of a car and another hanging out of the driver's side door. Then the bus sped up, leaving the grisly scene behind. Everyone was quiet; there just wasn't much to say. We all sat with our own thoughts about crime and death. In a few hours, we were at the bus station in Spencer, West Virginia.

A room at the Spencer Hotel cost a dollar, and their dining room was still open. The special was meatloaf, mashed potatoes, peas and carrots, and coffee. Wiley and I talked about the shootout at the border.

"If they had surrendered, they would go to jail for five years and still be alive," Wiley said.

"I guess they thought that they could get away," I said, "but the police are getting tougher on robbers since the FBI got involved." I wrote Kate another letter telling her about the bank robbers and that Wiley and I were never in danger.

In the morning, we asked the desk clerk where the sweet potato farm was. "The biggest one is Simmons farm ten miles east on the highway." A salesman gave us a ride, dropping us off at the farm.

Tully Simmons wrote our names in his book and asked, "Have you bagged sweet potatoes before?" I told him about Talbot's farm in Benton. And the two-by-four stands that made things easier and faster. "How long would it take to make them?" he asked.

"With a good carpenter, just a few hours," I said.

"Wait here, I'll be right back," he said. He was back in ten minutes with another man. "This is my handyman, David. You tell him what to build."

David took me to his work shed, and I explained how the stands were made. In an hour, he had one ready. "If this works, I'll build another," he said. It worked perfectly.

Tully was all smiles. "I won't forget this," he said.

It took two and a half weeks to bring in and bag the sweet potatoes. "Those new stands cut almost a week off the bagging," Tully told me. "I don't know why I never thought of it before."

Eddie Blake, another bagger, told me about the pumpkin farm in Elkins, West Virginia. "Elmer Dickens raises 350 acres of pumpkins and squash every year," he said, "and they got a heated bunkhouse."

Tully paid us on a Thursday afternoon. Opening my pay envelope, I found an extra five dollars with a small note that read 'Thanks!' Wiley and I got a ride into Spencer and went directly to the hotel. We were grubby and needed a shave and a bath. Our clothes were close to being rags.

I asked the desk clerk about a secondhand store. "Don't have one in town," he said, "but Phipp's Department store

146

is going out of business. Lots of clothes, real cheap." We got directions and left.

We got shirts for a quarter each, pants for fifty cents, and underwear ten cents a package. Wiley and I stocked up and went back to the hotel. It's amazing how a bath, a shave, and some clean clothes can make the world seem a better place.

"Don't forget, you owe Mattie and Kate a letter," I reminded Wiley.

"After we eat and see another movie," Wiley told me. Red beans and rice with lots of sausage was the special. I ate like a starving dog, washing it down with hot coffee. At the Temple theatre, we saw a western called 'The Big Trail' with a new star named John Wayne. Back at the hotel, we both wrote letters. I told Kate we would make one more stop at Plum, Pennsylvania, then we were coming home.

Bus tickets to Plum cost a dollar fifty each. As Wiley and I settled in for the ride, I asked him, "What do you plan to do when we get back to New Jersey?"

Giving me his most serious look, he told me, "Your brother-in-law Thomas said he could get me into the police Cadet training program. I have thought it over for months and have decided to become a policeman." I just sat there with my mouth open. I should have seen this coming, but it was still a surprise!

"Are you sure this is what you want?" I asked.

Then Wiley explained. "The traveling we have done is fine up to a point," he said, "because when the work is done, we can move on to a new job in a new place. But it's the same thing, day after day, like in a factory, it's boring, like a slow death."

"You want steady work with some excitement," I said.

"That is just what I want," Wiley said, "and being a cop will give me exactly that."

I closed my eyes and tried to picture Wiley in a uniform. It was blurry, but it was there.

"What do you plan to do?" Wiley asked.

Thinking a moment, I said, "I have some ideas, but must talk to Kate first." Wiley and I both knew this would be our last migrant adventure. Living on the road, moving from harvest to harvest, was exciting, but it was also sometimes dangerous and often dull. As Wiley said, the same work in different places.

CHAPTER THIRTY-FIVE

Emmett Castle was indeed glad to see us. "The potatoes have just started coming in and I need baggers. I can pay you each a dollar fifty a day." We went right to work. One hundred pound bags again. Three other pairs of men filling the burlap bags as fast as the potatoes came in. This time the work had meaning. It meant that when the potatoes and carrots were all bagged and loaded, Wiley and I would be going home.

By the third week of October, Emmett's fields were cleared. "This is our last trip," I told Emmett. "We are going home for good."

"Both of you have been good workers," he told us. "Thank you for a fine job." One of the produce truckers offered us a ride to Pittsburgh to catch the train to New Jersey. He dropped us off a block from the depot and waved goodbye. We bought our coach tickets for Trenton.

"Train leaves in an hour," said the clerk. At the station café, we got ham and cheese sandwiches and coffee. A man sitting near us looked about as rough as we did. Probably another migrant, I thought. Looking around, I saw several like Wiley and I. Men on the move, trying to make enough money to get a meal and a place to sleep.

Wiley and I boarded the train, bound for home. Wiley was soon asleep with his hat over his face. I stared into space with thoughts of Kate and the future ahead. As soon as I had steady employment, we could plan our wedding. An apartment would have to be our first home together, then a house to raise children in. All these plans would only come about with a regular job to support us. I could join the police force as Wiley intended to, but that was not a career to take lightly, just hoping that something better would come along. I knew Kate would have some ideas.

As it always had been in the past, the steady rolling motion soon put me to sleep. I woke with Wiley elbowing me in the ribs. "We are coming into the Trenton station," he said excitedly.

It was evening, and the air smelled like October, crisp and cold. Standing on the station platform, I said, "Let's go the YMCA first. We can get a room and clean up before we go home."

"A hot shower and clean clothes would suit me fine," Wiley said.

We got a room each for two dollars a week. They threw away the clothes I had been wearing, remembering Mattie's warning: 'I don't wash rags.' As I shaved, I realized I needed another haircut. As a migrant, personal grooming was a luxury. No one else cared how you looked, just whether you showed up and did your share of the work. We left the YMCA and started our walk to Sean and Mattie's house.

Knock, knock. Patrick opened the door, stared a few seconds, then shouted, "It's Uncle Wiley and Danny!" The family came running from all directions: Sean, Mattie, Liam, and my lovely Kate. Handshakes, hugs, and kisses followed. Kate and I held each other so tight we both could hardly breathe. I loved it.

Everyone wanted our first-hand account of the hurricane. Sean brought out the newspaper stories they had saved with pictures of the damage. There was a picture of the 'Viola' lying on the beach. By ten in the evening, the coffee was gone, and the boys were in bed. It was Friday, so no work for Kate tomorrow.

Holding me close before we left, Kate said, "Tomorrow morning we need to get some proper clothing and shoes for you. I have someone who wants to meet you, and you should make a good impression."

Nine o'clock Saturday morning found us at Piper's Department store. My old boots went into the trash and were replaced with some comfortable black shoes. A white dress shirt was next, followed by a tie and a dark gray sport coat. Looking in the full-length mirror, I could hardly believe it was me! As we paid the bill and left, I said, "We must be meeting someone very special."

"Let's stop at the lunch counter for a quick coffee," Kate said, "and I will tell you all about it." Sitting at the end of the counter sipping coffee, Kate began her story. "From your first letter, I knew you had a talent for telling stories. You made me feel as if I were there with you, living the tale."

"I was only writing what I saw and felt," I said.

Giving me her most lovely smile, Kate continued. "When you left on your second adventure, I took some of your letters to the editor of the Trenton Times. I asked him to read them carefully and I would return in two days. On my second visit Mr. Seebold, the editor, told me that when you returned, he wanted to meet with you about a possible position at the paper as a writer!" I just stared at Kate for a minute, not knowing what to say.

"I know the letters were meant only for me," she said, "but you have a talent given to you by God. Not to share it with everyone would be to deny that gift." A light shimmer of moisture in her eyes told of possible tears.

Taking both her hands in mine, I said softly, "There are times when saying 'I love you' just doesn't begin to express what I feel. Let's go meet this editor and see what happens."

Mr. Seebold was a medium-tall man with an unruly thatch of gray hair and wore bifocals. We shook hands and sat in chairs facing his desk, behind which he sat looking at me over his glasses.

"Have you ever taken a journalist course in High School?" he asked.

"No sir," I said. "I was busy working."

He leaned forward, elbows on his desk, toying with a yellow pencil. "When Miss Bishop bought me your letters, I didn't expect much, just another young man's letters to his sweetheart. Then I took them home and really read them." He tilted his head to one side and smiled. "You took me on a journey to places I will never go and had me see things I will never see, and made me feel I was there with you."

He dropped the pencil and laid his hands flat on his

desk. "I want you to come to work for the Trenton Times. You will start as a copy boy and learn the trade." I thought I was going to faint but managed to remain upright in my chair. "Your pay will start at $20 per week. Meanwhile you must fulfill two requirements."

Holding one finger in the air, he said, "You must take a journalism course at the local college. There is one starting next week." The second finger went up. "You must also learn to use a typewriter. The college also has that course. Can you do these things?"

"Feeling my strength coming back, I answered, "I will register for both classes today, and thank you."

"Thank the wise young lady next to you," he said, "and I would like to send a reporter around to your house this afternoon to do a story on your survival of the hurricane in Florida."

Kate and I walked in silence from the building. When we reached the sidewalk, and the lobby door swung closed behind us, I threw my hands as high in the air as high as they could go and yelled at the top of my lungs, "Thank you God for bringing this wonderful, beautiful woman into my life! I love her!" Kate was laughing and crying at the same time. We hugged, and I picked her up and twirled her around, then set her down and kissed her gently.

Looking into her glistening eyes, I said, "If I reached into your pocket right now I bet I would find directions to the Junior College." Still laughing, Kate dipped her hand into her coat pocket and pulled out a piece of paper.

"We can take the bus," she said.

CHAPTER THIRTY-SIX

Arriving home about three in the afternoon, Wiley greeted us at the door. Seeing our flushed faces and big smiles, he asked, "And what silliness have you two been up to today?"

"Let's go inside and we will tell you," said Kate. Mattie was baking bread and stirring a large pot of something that gave off a delicious aroma. Kate told them of our visit to the Trenton Times, the job offer, and the college enrollment. We all hugged, laughed, and the women cried a bit. Then Wiley broke his news about joining the police force! More crying and hugging. Amid this, there was a loud knock on the door. I opened it, and there stood a lovely young woman. Her slender figure, auburn hair, and blue eyes made me wonder if God were tempting me with her beauty.

Holding out her hand, she said, "My name is Paula O'Neal, I work for the Trenton Times."

"Yes, of course," I said, inviting her in, "Mr. Seebold said he was sending a reporter to do a story on the hurricane." From the kitchen came Mattie, Kate, and Wiley. One look at Paula O'Neal and Wiley stopped in his tracks. With eyes wide, he looked like someone who had been hit in the head with a mallet. Miss O'Neal was not doing much better. Her hand was shaking slightly as she held it out to Wiley. When their hands touched, I swear there was a spark of electricity between them.

Neither Mattie, Kate, nor I had ever seen this reaction from Wiley when meeting a pretty girl. "Miss O'Neal is here to do a story on our miraculous survival of the Clearwater hurricane," I said.

Gathering her professional self together, Paula said, "The paper has the overall story well covered, but you two men were actually there. I want to get down on paper what you went through." Sitting on the wing-back chair, Paula took a large notepad from her bag. "Start from the beginning of the storm and if I have any questions I will hold up my hand."

Kate and I sat quietly as Wiley unfolded the story. As he spoke, I saw it again in my mind. Paula stopped Wiley twice to ask me questions, but her attention was on Wiley.

When the story ended, Paula said, "This may be the best story I have covered thus far in my short career."

"How long have you been a reporter?" Wiley asked.

"I have been with the Times for two years," Paula said. "This is my third big coverage."

Sensing an opening, I asked Paula, "Would you like to do another story related to this one?"

"And what would that be?" she asked.

"Wiley is going off to the Police Academy to become a police officer," I told her. "Following him through his training program might make a story in itself."

I saw Paula's eyes light up at the possibilities. "I will mention it to Mr. Seebold," she said. "I don't believe we have ever done anything on police training. It would make a wonderful story." She handed Wiley a card. "This is how you can reach me at the paper if you think of anything you may have missed." Shaking hands all around, Paula left with a little spring in her step.

Sunday morning Wiley, Kate, and I took the bus to Queens to visit Thomas and Amy. It was a happy occasion with all the good news about my new job.

Thomas brought out some papers for Wiley to sign. "Your training will last six months," he said. "You will report to the training facility tomorrow morning and live at the police barracks. Training is every day except Sunday." Wiley told him about Paula and the possibility of a news story about police training.

"I will take this news to my Captain who will set it all up with the Police Commissioner," Thomas said, "and I am sure he will love the idea."

On the ride home, Kate hugged my arm and said, "Amy and I want to bring the two families together. I am going to ask Mattie to have everyone at our house for Thanksgiving dinner."

"It's a wonderful idea," I said. "Patrick and Liam will have new laps to sit on." I asked Wiley, "Is there a remote possibility that a Miss Paula O'Neal may join us on that day?"

With a tender smile, Wiley replied, "I will give that possibility my utmost attention."

I reported for work Monday morning, not quite sure what to expect. Against the far wall of the newsroom was a long wooden bench. I learned this was to be my office, alongside four other young men also learning the trade. When one of the writers or reporters yelled 'boy,' one of us responded. Our duty was to move the written copy from the rewrite desk to the city desk or from the city desk to the copy desk. When the edited copy was ready, it went to the composing room, where it was set up to be printed. When the presses were running, you could feel it throughout the entire building, a vibration that made your blood hum and your teeth grind.

When we were not moving the copy, we were all gofers. Cries of 'I need coffee' or 'get me some cigarettes' rang out through the room. Often, if a reporter were doing a lengthy story, a gofer would be sent to the local Deli for sandwiches. By the end of the week, I knew this was the kind of work I would like. Getting the story was only the beginning. How you presented the story to the public was the true test of a good reporter.

My workday was over at five. I then had half an hour to catch the cross-town bus to the college. My first class was Journalism with Professor was Mr. Julius 'just-call-me-Sir' Kalmon. He opened his first class by telling us what a journalist was and was not.

"A journalist relates to the public a tale of truth," he said. "You must tell the tale as it is, not how you wish it to be. There is no side for you to take in the telling, only a true journalist will be able to detach themselves enough to stay out of the story. This class will teach you to take the reader with you as you tell of good deeds, bad deeds, life, death and all that makes up our world."

I learned to use new words, sentence structure, paragraphs, commas, and other punctuation to make a story readable.

CHAPTER THIRTY-SEVEN

I believe two inventions changed our world: the telephone and the typewriter. I often had to answer the telephone in the copy room. I soon realized that I did not have to yell into the receiver to be heard. If I did yell, the person on the other end would yell back and tell me to stop yelling! Mattie and Sean were soon having one installed in their home. The YMCA where I was living had one at their desk. After a fashion, the phone and I became friends.

The typewriter was one of those things you looked at and wondered how it could ever work. My first typewriter class was taught by Miss Pringle, a gray-haired forty-something who never smiled, ever. You only knew she was in a good mood if she was not frowning.

In our class, there were six women and two men. The other man was younger and very self-confident. He and the women mastered the keyboard in a week. I was not so fortunate. There is a certain way to hold your hands above the keyboard for ease of operation. I will master this someday.

Also, I learned to type looking at a paper or a book, not at the keyboard. The Lord knows I tried. To some degree, I was able to accomplish this with less than ten mistakes. My large hands also got me into trouble.

"The keyboard is not an enemy to be vanquished," Miss Pringle would remind me as she stood over me, shaking her head. I was determined to master this machine. It would serve me well to sit down at any typewriter and do in minutes what a hand holding a pencil would take an hour.

I often finished class too late to visit Kate in the evening. I would drag myself to my room, undress, and fall into bed. My work schedule was structured to give me every other Saturday off. On those days, Kate and I would plan something special.

One Saturday, Kate and I chased Mattie and the boys out of the house, giving them tickets to the zoo. While they were gone, we cleaned the house and made supper. Another Saturday, we went to two museums and an art show. We talked of when we would marry and who to invite, decided on flowers and compromised on which church. We held off setting a date until I completed my schooling, holding tightly to the fact that it would happen.

One Sunday morning, there was a knock on my door. I opened it, and there stood Wiley, dressed in his police cadet uniform and looking splendid! We laughed and hugged.

"Aren't you the well-dressed young cop," I said.

"I am doing so well I earned a one day pass to visit family," he said.

"Let's go visit Mattie and Kate." As we walked, I asked, "Have you kept in touch with Miss Paula O'Neal?"

"I have," Wiley said. "The Times is going to do a full length story on police training. The first segment begins next week in the Sunday edition, followed by four more segments, on Sunday's. Paula is doing the writing." I filled Wiley in on my classes at college.

Laughing, he said, "In the future, when I am having a difficult day, I will think of you learning to use the typewriter."

Wiley's visit was the high point of our Sunday. At noon, Sean took Patrick and Liam to pick out pumpkins for the upcoming Halloween. I decided to ask Kate a question that had been preying on my mind for some time.

"I remember Wiley telling me that your father was in jail for assaulting a Judge," I said. "Will he be out soon?" Mattie, Kate, and Wiley looked at each other a long moment, then Kate spoke. "The three of us made a pact years ago not to speak of our father," she said, "but with you now being a family member you really must know the truth."

Taking my hands in hers, she continued. "Our father, William, is in prison, In Ireland." Kate was gripping my hand tightly. "After our mother's death, father spent much time in one of the local pubs with his friends. Many of them were avid supporters of those trying to free Ireland from English rule."

"It was the drink that ruined him," injected Mattie.

Nodding her head in agreement, Kate said, "Yes, the drink had much to do with it. One day, father came home and told us he was going to Ireland to join in the fight." Wiley gave Mattie a hug, and she wiped the tears from her face with the corner of her apron.

"We got one letter from him telling us he had joined the Irish Republican Army," Wiley said, "and then nothing from him for a year."

In her calm voice, Kate said, "The next letter was from father's Attorney asking for money, which we did not have. Father was being held in jail on suspicion of murder. Someone from the IRA had planted a bomb outside the British soldiers barracks. Three soldiers were killed, many more wounded." Kate now had tears in her eyes. "Three men, including father, were arrested for the bombing. All were convicted of murder. At the sentencing, father jumped the railing and attacked the Judge."

"His temper was always on a short fuse," Mattie said.

Placing his hand on my shoulder, Wiley said, "My sisters and I agreed to keep this gruesome event in the past and never speak of it. Only two outsiders know. Mattie's husband Sean, and now you." I was stunned!

"You have my word it will go no further," I said, "but I am glad you confided in me. Do Patrick and Liam know?"

Slowly shaking her head, Mattie said, "the boys only know their grandfather is alive and living in Ireland. Perhaps, when they are older, they will be told the full truth." The four of us stood, and we all hugged together.

Sean and the boys returned with four pumpkins, two for carving and two for pies later. We placed the newspaper on the kitchen table, and many hands went to work gutting and carving gap-toothed faces on the big orange pumpkins. A roasted chicken was supper that night.

Later, as Wiley and I waited for his bus back to the police barracks, I asked, "When is your training completed?"

"The last week of April, next year I will get my badge," he said. "And when are your college courses done?"

Laughing, I told him, "The last week of April, next year."

CHAPTER
THIRTY-EIGHT

I arrived early at the Hudson Street home of Sean and Mattie Flanagan. I wanted to help in any way I could because my sister Amy and her husband Thomas O'Riley would be joining us for Thanksgiving dinner. It would be the first meeting of the two families. Kate had arranged it with Amy and Thomas, who were anxious to meet the Flanagan family. A sixteen-pound turkey was on the kitchen table. Kate was stuffing a mixture from a bowl into the big bird while Mattie stirred a pot on the stove.

Seeing me, Mattie smiled. "You arrived just in time." Pointing at a stack of potatoes on the counter. "Those potatoes must be peeled and cut up to boil." I found a knife and got busy. Sean spent the night at the firehouse, and upon arriving home, was told by Mattie to change clothes and then take the boys to morning mass. Like any good husband, Sean complied.

Thomas and Amy got to the house at one that afternoon. Amy presented Mattie with two pies—one pumpkin and one apple. Soon after, Wiley arrived alone. "Paula's mother is in a nursing home," he told us. "Paula is spending the day with her and I will see her later."

By two in the afternoon, all was ready. We gathered around the table, and Sean led us in saying grace. It was a delicious meal. The turkey was done to perfection, as were the potatoes, gravy, stuffing, and green beans. Amy's pies were a big hit, with both Mattie and Kate wanting the secret for the flaky crust.

Later, the talk turned to family history, which is the backbone of Irish culture. Sean's family had their beginning in County Mayo on Ireland's west coast, and the Bishop family originated from County Wicklow on the east coast. The Broome family was still active in County Galway. As Thomas and Amy left that evening, they promised to have another gathering soon at their home.

After Kate's lingering kiss goodnight, Wiley and I walked to the bus stop. "I hope to see you and Paula soon," I said.

"Paula's father is dead and her mother is in her last stage of liver disease," he said. "She is not expected to make it to Christmas. After this sad event has passed, we will have more time together." As the bus took Wiley back to his barracks, I walked home to the YMCA. Tomorrow was a workday, and with a stomach full of turkey, I was soon asleep.

I caught glimpses of Paula on Friday as she put the finishing touches on her Sunday story. Around the newsroom rang out cries of 'copy!' One of us would jump from the bench to move the copy along. Then I heard a female voice yell 'copy!' I was on my feet and found the voice. It was Paula! Without looking up, she handed me the paper saying, "This goes to the copy desk."

"I'm on my way," I said. At the sound of my voice, she looked up, and her lovely face broke into a smile.

"Mr. Danny Broome! Wiley told me you were working here. How is the job going?"

"I am learning something each day," I said.

With a mischievous grin, Paula said, "Someday we must do lunch so you can tell me all about Wiley."

"It would be my pleasure," I said. "I am sure there are things he has not yet told you, like our wild ride with the moonshiner in Tennessee."

"That is a story I would very much like to hear," Paula said. "The more I learn about Wiley, the better."

About ten Saturday morning, I noticed the smoke. I was looking out the rear window of the Times building, and I saw a dark plume in the distance. There were other homes with smoke coming from their chimneys, but this was blacker with tiny burning embers. I grabbed the nearest reporter, a guy named Sam, and said, "I think that's a roof fire."

One look was enough for Sam. He yelled, "Fire around 54th street! Call the fire Department!"

Mr. Seebold stuck his head out of his office. "Sam, take Hughey and Danny with you. I want pictures." Tim Hughes, or Hughey as everyone called him, was the best news photographer in Trenton. He had the awards to prove it. I got my coat and ran after Sam with Hughey right behind me.

The old Methodist Church on 54th street was a landmark. One hundred and five years old, the structure was mostly stone, but the framework—floors, pews, and the belfry—were oak. When we arrived, two fire trucks were already pumping water onto the blazing roof.

Handing me one of his bags, Hughey said, "hold this while I get some shots." His flash camera in hand, Hughey got as close as he could and began taking pictures. Sam was talking to one of the firemen, nodding his head and taking notes. A crowd was gathering to watch, and I heard a man say, "This same thing happened about five years ago. They never clean the chimney before starting the furnace."

Another fire truck roared up, its siren blaring. Hoses were hooked up to hydrants, and steady streams of water poured onto the church roof. A ladder truck drove in from another direction, getting as close to the church as it could. I saw Sean Flanagan manning one of the hoses with two other firefighters.

Slowly the blaze receded, the smoke turning from dark gray to light gray. Hughey was everywhere at once, his flashbulbs popping with a bright light. Sam had found the fire Chief and was writing furiously as the chief spoke and pointed. In the space of two hours, the church had been saved. Now would come the clean-up and repairs.

Walking back to the newsroom, Sam said, "You will get some credit for this story. If you had not noticed the smoke when you did, the church may have been lost."

I heard Hughey say, "Look at this," and when I turned, he took my picture with that bright flash.

The story made the Sunday edition of the Times front page. A half-page picture of the fire with a much smaller photo of me. I was slightly embarrassed by it, but Kate said, "I am letting everyone at the bank know that you are my future husband and a hero."

I asked Sean how extensive was the damage. "The church will need a complete new roof and some repairs to the choir loft and belfry. It could have been much worse."

CHAPTER THIRTY-NINE

Mrs. Amanda O'Neal, mother of Paula O'Neal, died on December 3, 1931. The entire newsroom staff attended the funeral. Paula requested a closed casket; the liver disease had ravaged her mother's small body. Amanda had served briefly as a nurse during the Great War, and her country did not forget.

A flag-draped coffin was carried to the gravesite by six men in Army uniforms, and a twenty-one gun salute was fired. As the coffin was lowered, a bugler played taps. Wiley had managed to get a day off to attend. Without him by her side, I think Paula may have been overwhelmed.

The ladies from the Catholic Church Ladies Aid Society served coffee and sandwiches later in the church basement. Mattie and Kate got a promise from Paula to be at their home for Christmas. Ashes to ashes, dust to dust.

The journalism class revealed its secrets to me slowly, piece by piece. I learned to research the story before attempting to write it. The story must begin with something to catch the reader's eye, to make them want to keep reading. Background and location can be revealed as the story progresses. All these things and more made me look forward to each class. Professor Kalmon was very good at his job. He seemed to know whom to encourage and when. The formation of an idea was beginning in the back of my mind. I did not dwell on it but did not dismiss it either.

I had mastered the keyboard on the typewriter. I knew this because Miss Pringle no longer frowned while looking over my shoulder. I even got an occasional nod of approval. My spelling was improving as well as my use of punctuation. The brand of typewriters at the college was an Underwood. The Times newsroom used mainly Royals. When I asked old Sam why he said, "The Times has a contract with the Royal Company. A ten per cent discount on each machine for three years."

There was talk around the newsroom that Congress was considering ending prohibition. The great idea of no alcohol had turned into a nightmare. Organized crime had taken over the entire country, bringing in every kind of alcoholic beverage from Canada, Mexico, and every other nation. It came by truck, by boat, by any means available. Major crime families chopped up the larger cities into their private kingdoms. Trenton was no exception.

Like Chicago, New York, and Boston, Trenton had its problems with alcohol and crime. Two families, in particular, kept the police force busy—the D'Amico mob and the Badami family. Each wanted a bigger slice of the city to control. It was not unusual to read about an overnight gun battle or see pictures of dead bodies lying in the street. What was unusual was for two dead bodies to be found at the entrance of the Times newsroom building on a Sunday morning in December. The police responded to the call made by the janitor, who was the first to arrive that morning. The bodies were removed to the morgue. A reporter followed up on the deaths and discovered that although the men were from rival gangs, the murders were not crime-related but love-related. The article read:

"Antonio 'Tubby' Amolino, age 31, had just been released from a thirty day sentence in jail and could not find his lady friend, Teresa Bonatti. After searching several speakeasies he learned that the lovely, well-proportioned Teresa was now the lover of Salvatore 'Soso' Caranzano, age 32. The two men began searching the city of Trenton for each other. They finally met at three in the morning in front of the Times building. There were no words exchanged only gunfire. Both managed to get off two shots, and both died where they lay. Teresa Bonatti has apparently moved on and has not been heard from."

Christmas was a week away, and my shopping was almost complete. This year Amy and Thomas would be joining the Bishop and Flanagan families for Christmas dinner. Amy had wanted to hold the feast at her home, but there just wasn't enough room in their small house. Mattie and Kate planned to have a large ham glazed with a brown sugar sauce. I drooled whenever I thought of it.

The tree was up and trimmed, homemade paper garlands were strung over doorways, and a large wreath with a big red bow decorated the front door. The radio kept a constant flow of carols through the house. The aroma of sugar cookies and gingerbread flowed from the kitchen into every room. No holiday promises magic the way Christmas does.

Christmas morning at the Flanagan home was a day of peace and joy. The boys, Patrick and Liam, passed around the gifts. Tears and laughter mingled with the Christmas carols from the radio playing softly in the background. Wiley and Paula arrived bearing more gifts. Thomas and Amy soon were there, and the family was complete.

The meal was a huge success. The large ham disappeared slowly down to the bone, which would be saved for a savory soup. We shared stories from past Christmases and laid plans for the new year. An Easter buffet-style dinner at the home of Thomas and Amy was planned by Mattie, Kate, Amy, and Paula. Mattie was making sure that Amy would get her wish to have dinner at her home.

Later that night, back at my room at the YMCA, I said a long prayer of thank you to God for all the wonders I was feeling.

1933 brought wonderful news. Prohibition was to be repealed! The great experiment that had gone so wrong would be over. President Hoover would sign the amendment in February, and taverns and pubs across America would once again open their doors. Restaurants could serve wine with meals, and the breweries and distilleries could hire people back to work. The new Banking Act would go into effect in March. Banks across America were hit hard by the depression. The banking act would prevent future bank closings by loaning Federal money to the banking system. A new President was in charge.

CHAPTER FORTY

The dust storms in the Midwest were becoming a national disaster. Wiley and I had witnessed the beginning of this tragedy while working in Kansas and Nebraska. Daily headlines told of families wiped out by the storms. People were packing what few belongings they had and moving to California to find work. Hobo camps sprang up alongside railroad tracks. Men with no job and no future rode the rails looking for a better life.

Bank robberies became a way of life for some. Every day, the headlines boldly told their story. Arthur 'Pretty Boy' Floyd, John Dillinger, Vern Miller, Lester Gillis, also known as 'Baby Face' Nelson, the Barker Gang, Bonnie and Clyde, and many more terrorized the country with their daring exploits. Trenton, New Jersey had its own problems with a young couple named Jake and Lucy Popeck. Using a stolen car, they managed to rob four banks in one week. Bank number five did not go as planned.

I was sitting at my desk (the bench against the wall) when the call came into the newsroom. Carl Ackers, a seasoned reporter, answered the phone, scribbled something on a notepad, hung up, and yelled, "Trenton Bank and Trust is being robbed!"

Mr. Seebold stuck his head out of his office and yelled, "Carl, Sam, get Hughey and get over there." The three men left the newsroom on the run. The driver of a newspaper delivery van was pressed into service and drove them to the scene.

Two hours later, they all returned looking very somber. As Sam and Carl compared notes and began drafting the story, they related the events.

"These two crazy kids came storming into the bank yelling, "Everyone get down on the floor, this is a robbery!' All the customers got down on the floor except one guy." Checking his notes, Sam added, "The guy standing was there to rob the bank also! He pulled a gun and shot the woman, Lucy Popeck!"

Carl picked up the story. "Jake Popeck turned around and shot the man who shot his wife, then went to her to see how badly she was hit."

Sam took over. "The man Jake shot, shot Jake, and then slowly sank to the floor, dead."

Carl finished the story. "The police came running in, saw Jake with a gun and shot him. All three robbers died there on the bank floor." Together Sam and Carl interviewed the police and learned the man who killed the Popeck's was a known felon named Alden Schwab, who was wanted in two other robberies in New Jersey. None of the other bank customers were injured, and no money was taken.

I passed my typewriter class and was awarded a certificate of completion. Miss Pringle did not smile as she handed out these awards, but she did not frown either. In another month, the Journalism class would have a final exam. Part of the final was to write about an event in our past that made an impression on us. I chose the fire in the hayfield and the mad dash to the river with the horses. I asked Kate for the letter I had sent her telling her about the fire. We sat and read the letter together.

"Close your eyes and picture the day in your mind," she said. As my eyes closed, I remembered the drought and the hot, dusty wind. I could almost smell the sweat from the horses and the feel of the hay beneath my feet. "This is going to be the best story," I told Kate.

I needed a typewriter of my own, but the problem was the cost. These were expensive machines, well beyond my means. A new Underwood cost $49.95, and a new Royal was $54.95. I would have to look for a good used one or a reconditioned one. Then my past came back to remind me that good deeds have a way of catching up to you.

Kate came home from work one afternoon and could hardly wait to tell me her news. "I met an old friend of yours today," she said, "a Mr. Franklin P. Dowd." I frowned as I searched my memory for this name, but nothing came to mind.

"How does he know me," I asked. Kate sat me down at the kitchen table and explained.

"I keep a picture of you on my desk," she said, "so you are with me all day, every day. This morning the bank examiner arrived, and we began going over the books. He noticed the picture of you and broke out smiling and laughing! 'That's the young man who saved my life,' he told me!" Then it hit me! The bank examiner on the train when I tackled the robber!

"I remember him now," I said. "He was so glad that we had saved his father's watch."

"Yes, and he wanted to know all about you," Kate said, "so he took me to lunch. I told him you were working at the newspaper and taking a class in Journalism. He wants very much to see you again, so I told him to call Mr. Seebold at the newsroom."

The next morning Mr. Seebold called me into his office. "Are you in any trouble at the bank," he asked me.

Startled, I replied, "No sir, of course not. Why do you ask?"

"The bank we do business with called me," he said. "They want you to be there at ten o'clock to meet with the bank examiner." I told Mr. Seebold the story of the train robbery and how the bank examiner was involved. Mr. Seebold settled back in his chair, chuckling, then began to laugh!

"Danny Broome, I remember running that story in our paper! Go to the bank, and take Paula and Hughey with you. I want pictures!"

The bank president, Mr. Alvin Jessup, Franklin P. Dowd, and Kate were waiting to greet us as we entered the bank. Mr. Dowd's smile spread from ear to ear as he shook my hand.

"I have thought of you many times over the past few years. I always hoped we would meet again," he said.

Mr. Jessup also shook my hand and said, "We have a surprise for you in the conference room." Kate took my hand and led me to the room, with Paula and Hughey following behind. On the long table in front of us sat two boxes with ribbons and bows on them. Franklin P. Dowd took the lead.

"As you know, I took your lovely fiancé to lunch and she told me all about your new career in Journalism. I have always wanted to show you my gratitude for the brave act you performed that day."

Pointing to the large box on the table, Mr. Dowd continued. "A professional journalist needs the proper equipment to further his career. This is my gift to you Danny Broome. Open it please." Hughey had already taken three pictures, and Paula was taking notes. With shaking hands, I removed the bow and ribbon and opened the box. In all its beauty sat a new Royal typewriter! I felt tears forming at the corners of my eyes as I stroked the keys. Kate's small hand slipped into mine as she hugged my arm. Hughey flashed more pictures as Paula patted my back.

Sensing my discomfort, Mr. Jessup spoke up. "The bank would like to add to this most generous gift with a little something of our own," he said as he pushed the smaller box toward me. I opened it to reveal several reams of paper, some additional ribbons, and a card signed by the bank employees.

"I will never forget this," I told Mr. Dowd.

Smiling, he said, "This has bought me more pleasure than you can ever know. Thank you Mr. Danny Broome."

The newspaper did run the story on page three. Mr. Seebold had found the original story of the foiled train robbery and passed it around the newsroom. Hughey gave me one of the pictures he had taken of Mr. Dowd, Kate, me, and the Royal.

CHAPTER FORTY-ONE

The young Irishman who had asked me to buy him a cup of coffee over two years ago now stood before us, accepting his new badge. It was the graduating class of police cadets looking smart and trim in their new uniforms. The entire family had turned out with Paula to witness this grand event. Thomas O'Riley was up front with the welcoming group of police; Amy was with the family. Wiley had become like another brother to her. She dabbed at her eyes with a handkerchief as she watched Wiley receive his badge. Mattie, Kate, and Paula were sniffling and hugging each other. Patrick held my left hand, and Liam had my right.

The truly amazing event had happened the night before. Sean, Mattie, and I were in the kitchen having coffee and sampling Mattie's latest batch of molasses cookies when Wiley and Paula showed up.

"I have some news for all of you," Wiley said with his usual smile. "This evening, Miss Paula O'Neal has agreed to become my wife." Mattie and Kate both screamed! Paula was laughing and crying as she showed everyone her engagement ring. Patrick and Liam, who had been in the living room listening to the radio, came running to find out what the screams were all about. Hugs and handshakes dominated the kitchen as the family 'oohed' and 'aahed' over the ring.

"We have not yet set a date," Wiley said, "but we have discussed the possibility of a double wedding with Danny and Kate."

My beautiful and sensible Kate said, "it is a grand idea Wiley, but I must decline. Each woman wants her very own wedding day. It is special to her and her husband. Two weddings together would take something away from that most precious moment in a woman's life."

Paula spoke up. "Kate is right. We each want that day as our own. The pictures and memories will be cherished forever as the day two became one."

After the graduation ceremony was over, we all met at the Hudson street home to celebrate. Taking Wiley to one side, I told him about the reunion with Franklin P. Dowd and the Royal typewriter.

Laughing, Wiley said, "Your rough and rowdy past caught up with you, now I expect you to put that machine to good use."

Kathryn Ellen Bishop became Mrs. Daniel Broome on the first day of June 1933. She was the most beautiful bride I had ever seen. The church was half-filled with family and friends. Mattie was her Matron of Honor with Amy and Paula as bridesmaids. Wiley, of course, was my best man, with Sean and Thomas in attendance. I don't recall much of the ceremony. I was still in awe that this lovely talented woman wished to spend the rest of her life with me.

The reception was held in the church basement with a beautiful cake baked and iced by Mattie and Amy. We received one gift, but it was the best gift imaginable. Sean and Mattie, Thomas and Amy, and Wiley and Paula had pooled their resources to pay the first month's rent on a small house on Beech Street, only two blocks from Sean and Mattie. The house came with four furnishings—a double bed, a kitchen table, and two chairs. More would be added when the budget allowed. I cannot describe our wedding night. It was a magical time of discovery for both of us. No more walking to my lonely room each night dreaming of this. We were now one, forever.

Wiley and Paula had set a wedding date for June 28th. Again, all the family would be in attendance. Meanwhile, Kate and I had been busy adding furnishings to our house—purchasing a sofa and two easy chairs from an estate sale. More chairs were added to the kitchen, and we hung pictures on the walls.

Tyler Holdren called one Saturday afternoon. "We are doing some redecorating at the YMCA," he said, "and I wondered if you would have any use for a dresser and a desk at your home."

"Thank you for thinking of us," I said. "Those are two things we could certainly use." Tyler had a truck drop them off at our house. Kate immediately had the desk placed in the corner of the living room. "This will be your special corner where you create your work," she said. I put my Royal typewriter on the desk and sat there staring at it. Standing behind me, Kate placed her hands on my shoulders.

"You have been wanting to write a book about your

travels," she said softly. "Now would be a good time to start." I had the idea of a book in the back of my mind since my first week in the college journalism class. I had never mentioned it to Kate, but somehow, she knew. She left for a moment and returned with all the letters I had written her bound with a white ribbon.

Handing me the bundle, she said softly, "All the letters you wrote me are here. Much of your journey with Wiley is here, the rest is waiting in your memory."

Staring at the typewriter, I asked, "Where do I start?"

"You must think back to when your life changed," Kate said. My thoughts raced back to the morning I got the handbill while waiting in the bread line. As if reading my mind, Kate said, "Your story starts when you decide to go to Plum, Pennsylvania to plant potatoes and carrots. Do you remember that day?" I did. Placing my fingers on the typewriter keys, I began my story . . .

The bread and soup line seems to get longer every morning. More jobs gone, more men out of work, and more families going hungry. Last year, 1929, the stock market crashed, and the whole country went belly up. My name is Danny Broome, and I worked for the Compton Coal Company delivering fifty-pound bags of coal to homes in the Bronx, New York. I stand almost six feet tall and can carry a bag of coal on each shoulder. My dark hair and dark hazel eyes let you know I am an Irishman.

The End

ABOUT THE AUTHOR

———

Mark Gengler was born and raised on a small farm north of Medford, Wisconsin. He joined the U.S. Army in 1963 and was stationed at Fort Bragg, N.C., with the 82nd Airborne Division. He saw action in the Dominican Republic in 1965. After his discharge, he traveled America, working odd jobs in California, Texas, Colorado, Kansas City and New Orleans. He returned to Wisconsin and went to broadcasting school on the G.I. Bill. Mr. Gengler was a disc-jockey, got married, and went to work at the University of Wisconsin, Oshkosh, until retiring in 2003.

———